TALES FOR THE MIDNIGHT HOUR

*Volume
Two*

TALES FOR THE MIDNIGHT HOUR

Volume
Two

J.B. STAMPER

SCHOLASTIC INC.
New York Toronto London Auckland Sydney
Mexico City New Delhi Hong Kong Buenos Aires

Still More Tales for the Midnight Hour, ISBN 0-590-45345-9,
Copyright © 1989 by J.B. Stamper. *Tailypo* and *Wait Till
Max Comes* are retellings of classic American folk stories.

Even More Tales for the Midnight Hour, ISBN 0-590-44143-4,
Copyright © 1991 by J.B. Stamper. *The Golden Arm* and *King
of the Cats* are retellings of classic American folk stories.

12 11 10 9 8 7 6 5 4 3 2 1   5 6 7 8 9/0

Printed in the U.S.A.   01

This edition created exclusively for Barnes & Noble, Inc.
2005 Barnes & Noble Books

ISBN 0-7607-6776-9

First compilation printing, April 2005

Contents

STILL MORE TALES FOR THE MIDNIGHT HOUR

Contents

Cemetery Road

Susan looked up at the sign on the corner of her new street: Cemetery Road. At the end of the block she could see the cemetery — row after row of tombstones behind a high iron gate. Susan knew the view well by now. It was the same view she had from her bedroom window.

Just a month ago, she'd lived in a pretty house with a view of a park. Then her father had been transferred to this city. And the only house they could afford was on Cemetery Road. Susan's friends had laughed when she gave them her new address. They thought she was joking.

"Hey, aren't you the new girl?" a voice called out from behind her.

Susan turned around to see two boys and one girl riding on bicycles. She recognized them from school. They were in some of the same classes with her.

Susan nodded her head in answer to their question and kept walking.

"What's it like living on Cemetery Road?" one of the boys asked. "Pretty spooky?"

Susan felt a flush creep into her cheeks. "Not at all," she said. "I'm not one bit afraid of living here."

The girl and the boys kept riding their bikes beside Susan as she walked quickly toward her house.

"I guess you haven't heard the stories about that cemetery," the girl said. "It's haunted by a black cat."

"Sure," Susan said. "Do you expect me to believe that?"

"It's true," the other boy said. "There's a big tomb in the middle of the graveyard — it has a statue of a black cat on top of it."

"What's so scary about that?" Susan asked.

"The cat comes alive at night," the girl said. "And haunts the cemetery."

"I don't believe in things like ghosts," Susan said.

"I dare you to visit the black cat at night," one of the boys said.

Susan glared at them. "I wouldn't be afraid to do that."

"Dare you to take off its collar," the girl said. "It has a leather collar around its neck, just like a real cat."

"Bring that collar to school tomorrow," the other boy said, "and you'll prove how brave you are."

"Dare you," the girl taunted.

"It's a dare," Susan said.

She ran away from their mocking faces toward her house. She would show them that she wasn't afraid. But the thought of going into the graveyard at night made her shudder. She had to get the collar this afternoon, before it got too dark out.

Susan's house was the second from the end of the road that led into the cemetery. A rickety old house that no one lived in sat right next to the graveyard. Susan pushed open the door to her house, went inside, and threw her books onto the bench in the hallway.

Before she could run up to her room to change, her mother rushed into the hallway. She told Susan that they were meeting her father at his office and then going out to dinner. Susan tried to protest, but it did her no good. Ten minutes later, she was driving downtown with her mother, worrying about when she would go to the cemetery.

They didn't come home until 10:00 that night. Susan went up to her room, put on her pajamas, and nervously stared out the window. The tombstones in the graveyard were bathed in the eerie light of the moon. Susan wondered how she would find the black cat there.

Finally her mother came in to say good night. Susan lay on her bed, waiting for the house to fall silent. When at last everything was quiet, she looked at the clock. It was 11:38.

Susan slipped out of her pajamas and into a T-shirt and jeans. Outside her screen window, the September night was still warm. She picked up the flashlight she used for camping trips and quietly stole down the stairs and out of the house.

Susan crept through the darkness past the rickety old house next to the graveyard and then through the arched entrance to the cemetery. She was afraid to use her flashlight in case someone in a nearby house saw her. The full moon shed enough light on the white gravel path for her to find her way in the dark.

Suddenly the stillness in the cemetery was broken by the weird call of a night bird. Susan froze in her steps. Until now, she had not been afraid. But the call reminded her that other things were out there in the night, watching her. She switched on her flashlight and swung it around it a wide circle. The beam lit up the cold, white marble tombstones around her.

Susan kept walking toward the middle of the cemetery, where the black cat was to be found. The gravel path sloped upward at a slight angle, and soon she found herself standing on a small hill. From the streetlights around the edge of the cemetery, she could tell she was near the center.

Susan shone the beam of the flashlight onto the nearby tombstones. The face of an angel stared back out of the darkness, making her catch her breath in fear. Then she saw it. The black cat was like a dark shadow in the night, crouching on top of a huge, white marble tomb.

Susan made her way on trembling legs over to the statue. The night bird shrieked again, sending a chill through her body. She stood underneath the cat and shone her light on it. The animal was made of smooth black marble, except for its eyes, which were of shining green stones. And around its neck, just as the girl had said, was a leather collar.

Susan climbed onto a step of the white base and read the inscription etched into the marble:

DISTURB NOT THE DEAD

For a second, she wanted to turn and run away, as fast as she could, from the tomb and its warning. But there, only inches from her hand, was the collar she had come to get.

She set down her flashlight beside the cat and reached both hands around its marble neck to unfasten the collar.

She whispered grateful thanks as its buckle came easily undone. But at that very moment, the bell on a nearby church began to strike the midnight hour. It frightened Susan so that she almost dropped the collar. On the fourth stroke of the bell, Susan picked up her flashlight and shone it into the cat's face. To her horror, the green eyes gleamed back at her like a real cat's. On the eighth stroke of the bell, Susan climbed down from the tombstone and heard a wicked hiss come from the statue. On the twelfth stroke of the bell, Susan ran down the gravel path of the graveyard, her heart in her throat and her mind in a frenzy of fear.

The light from the flashlight wavered on the path in front of her as Susan ran away from the black cat. She tried to tell herself that she had imagined the cat's hiss. But then, from behind her, she heard the soft thud of animal paws on the gravel path. And a long, angry hiss sounded through the night air. Susan turned around and saw what she feared. Two big green eyes were following her in the darkness.

Finally Susan reached the entrance to the cemetery. She could see her house ahead. It was only yards away now. She ran faster and faster until she reached the front door. With trembling hands she twisted open the knob and ran inside. She shut the door behind her, double-locked it, and then ran up the stairs, panting with fear.

She slipped into her bedroom and shut the door. From outside her screen window, she could hear a neighbor's dog howling weirdly in the night. Susan looked down at her trembling hands and saw the leather collar. Quickly she went to her dresser, opened the top drawer, and hid the collar inside. Then she put on her pajamas and lay down between the sheets, trembling with exhaustion and fear.

Susan stared out her window at the ghostly shapes of the tombstones in the moonlight. She listened to the dog's weird howl. And finally, after a long time, she fell into a fitful sleep.

Susan woke with a start. She had been having a terrible nightmare. In the dream, a black cat had been sitting on her chest, hissing down at her. Susan opened her eyes and stared into the darkness of her room. Then she remembered the collar. She switched on her lamp and ran to the dresser. Quickly she pulled out the top drawer.

The collar was gone.

Then Susan saw the deep claw marks of a cat on the top of the dresser. She whirled around and saw the big ragged hole torn in her window screen.

And there, on the windowsill outside, she saw the black cat . . . staring back at her with glowing green eyes.

The Wax Museum

"There's nothing to be scared of," the oldest boy in the class said in a bragging voice. "The people are just made of wax, like candles."

Still, the group of boys had slowed down to a shuffling pace, stepping on each other's heels and unconsciously herding together for safety. They were walking through the dimly lit entrance to the wax museum. Mr. Archer, their history teacher, was busy back at the admissions desk paying for their tickets.

"I hear this place has all the murderers in history," one young boy said nervously. "Hitler, even."

An uneasy giggle swept over the group. They had all heard stories about Hitler. What would he look like? Mr. Archer had said the wax figures seemed so real that you sometimes forgot they were wax.

Just as the boys came to a wooden door at the end of the hallway, Mr. Archer hurried up from behind them.

"All right, boys," he said in his deep, official voice. "We're ready to begin our tour. The museum director has agreed to let me take you around — since I've been here so often. Now everyone pair up and stand in a straight line."

There were a few minutes of pushing and shoving as the boys found partners and lined up. Mr. Archer looked over the group and noticed that, as usual, Andrew and Robbie had paired up together. He would have to watch them. But perhaps they would be good today, for once.

"Come along, then," Mr. Archer said importantly, opening the door in front of them to reveal a long, narrow room. An aisle ran down the center of the room, and on both sides were displays of people in historical costumes. The boys slowly filed in, their faces lit with amazement.

"They look so alive . . . it's creepy," a young boy said.

"There's Julius Caesar, being stabbed by

Brutus and his friends," one said, pointing his finger at a group of men in Roman togas.

"Ooh, look at the blood!" another boy said. "It still looks wet!"

Mr. Archer chuckled as the boys broke out of line and scrambled up to see the exhibits. Then he saw Andrew and Robbie standing together by the door, whispering to each other.

"Boys, come on in the room!" he said impatiently.

Andrew and Robbie stopped whispering and obediently walked up to the first exhibit. They stared down at Julius Caesar's body which was covered with knife wounds. Caesar's eyes were staring up at his murderers, and his face was twisted in the agony of death.

"This gives me the creeps," Robbie said.

"Not me. I think it's great." Andrew said. "It's like all these dead people have come alive again."

"You're weird," Robbie said.

"So is the museum," Andrew answered. "I wonder what we could do to add a little more excitement to this place."

Both boys turned to look at Mr. Archer, who was watching them with distrustful eyes.

"Why don't we just look at the exhibits?"

Robbie said, turning away from Caesar's bloody body. "I don't want to get into any trouble here."

Robbie stopped in front of another group of wax figures. In the center was Henry VIII, standing with his hands on his hips and his eyes staring straight ahead. Behind the king stood the wax figure of an executioner holding a double-edged ax in his hands. On the ground below him was the wax figure of Anne Boleyn, one of Henry VIII's wives. She was waiting to have her head chopped off at the orders of her husband, the king.

"Look at that ring on Henry's finger," Andrew whispered. "What a great souvenir it would be."

"Andrew!" Robbie said in a scared whisper. "Don't!"

But Andrew didn't pay any attention to him. He checked to see if Mr. Archer and the other boys were looking. Most of them had walked farther on down the aisle of exhibits. Andrew reached his hand out toward the king's left hand. He touched the cold wax of the fingers. Then he put his fingers around the ring and tugged at it. It slipped down a bit, but got stuck over the finger's waxy knuckle.

"Andrew, Robbie!" Mr. Archer's voice called from down the aisle. "Don't lag behind. Come along."

Andrew quickly pulled his hand away from the ring. He glanced up at the wax image of King Henry's face before leaving. The hard eyes were staring straight at him. They even seemed to follow him as he walked away.

"This place might be getting to me," Andrew said to Robbie. "I thought old Henry looked a little angry."

"You're going to get us into trouble," Robbie mumbled.

Andrew looked at him with a sneer. "You're turning out to be some coward, Robbie. Maybe I should get a new friend."

Robbie shook his head so hard that his glasses almost fell off. Andrew was his only friend. The two boys walked down the aisle to catch up with Mr. Archer and the rest of the class.

"Who knows the name of this great man?" Mr. Archer asked as he pointed toward a short man in military uniform standing in front of a map of Europe. The man had a scowl on his face and one hand pushed inside his jacket front.

"Napoléon Bonaparte, emperor of France," said the smartest boy in the class.

"That's correct," Mr. Archer said, beaming at the boy. "This is Napoléon, the great conquerer of Europe who was finally defeated at Waterloo. Now if you'll move along, we'll visit the more modern exhibits in the next room."

The class followed Mr. Archer through a set of heavy velvet curtains into the next room. Robbie started off after them, but Andrew pulled him back.

"Look what I just found," Andrew said, opening his hand to show Robbie something. Robbie peered down at the shiny piece of metal on his outstretched palm.

"It's a pin. Where did you get it?"

"I found it on the floor at home, just before I came here. I thought — "

"No!" Robbie said. "You can't do that. We'd be arrested. . . ."

"Calm down," Andrew said. "Nobody will ever know. I just want to find out if these things are really made of wax."

Andrew picked up the pin and leaned his long arm over the railing in front of the exhibit of Napoléon. He could just reach the emperor's left shoulder. With a quick jab, he pushed the pin through the costume and into the wax.

Robbie let out a short scream.

"Be quiet! What's the matter with you?" Andrew said, quickly pulling out the pin.

"Napoléon moved. I saw him move," Robbie stammered. "When you stuck that pin in, his face moved like it hurt."

Andrew looked at Robbie in disgust. "I can't believe you're such a coward. Look, you can see the wax on the pin. These people may look real, but they're just wax."

Robbie saw the coating of white wax on the pin. Then he looked again at Napoléon's face and ran off down the aisle to join Mr. Archer. Andrew trailed behind, hiding the pin in his pocket.

Mr. Archer was standing in a large round room that had exhibits all around its edges. He was telling the class a story. Robbie and Andrew just heard the end. " . . . and still today, we think of him as the monster of the twentieth century."

"Hitler," Robbie said and pointed to the man with a short mustache in a brown Nazi uniform.

"All right, boys," Mr. Archer said. "There

are many more interesting exhibits in this room. You can look around and ask me any questions you like." He paused and looked at his watch. "But in half an hour we'll be boarding the bus. I promised that I'd have you back in the school parking lot at three-fifteen."

"I don't have to be back," Andrew whispered to Robbie. "My parents are both away on vacation, and I'm staying at home alone."

"You're lucky your parents trust you," Robbie said.

"Especially since they shouldn't," Andrew added. "Let's take a closer look at Hitler."

The rest of the class was looking at different figures in the modern history room — Winston Churchill, Franklin D. Roosevelt, John F. Kennedy, Mahatma Gandhi, and others. Andrew and Robbie stood alone in front of the exhibit of Adolf Hitler and his Nazi officers.

"Even his mustache looks real," Robbie said, staring at Hitler's short, dark mustache.

"I wonder if it's made of real hair," Andrew said. "Turn around, Robbie, and keep a watch on everybody else. Tell me when they're not looking."

"What are you going to do?" Robbie asked in a worried voice.

"Just be quiet and tell me when nobody is looking," Andrew insisted.

Robbie watched nervously for a few minutes. Finally, the moment came when everyone's back was turned to them.

"Now!" he whispered.

Robbie turned around just as Andrew reached his hand out to Hitler's face and pulled at the hair of his mustache.

"It won't come loose!" Andrew hissed under his breath. He gave another hard tug.

Robbie screamed as Andrew's hand came back holding a small tuft of hair. Everyone in the room turned to stare at them.

"What's going on, boys?" Mr. Archer asked, hurrying over.

"Nothing, nothing, sir," Andrew said, hiding his hand behind his back.

"I thought I saw Hitler's hand move," Robbie stammered.

"He has a wild imagination," Andrew broke in to say.

Mr. Archer looked from Robbie to Andrew to the wax figure of Hitler. "Don't be ridiculous, Robbie, that is just a wax figure." Then he walked away, shaking his head.

"His hand did move, Andrew. . . ." Robbie

whispered in a scared voice. "Just when you pulled part of the mustache out. He started to hit you."

"Sure, Robbie, sure," Andrew said, ignoring his friend. "How do you like my souvenir?" He displayed the tuft of hair in his outstretched hand. "I just wish I had that ring on Henry the Eighth's finger." Suddenly, Andrew's face lit up with a smile. "I know what I'll do. And you've got to help me, Robbie."

"No, Andrew, forget it," Robbie said.

"Come on, all you have to do is tell Mr. Archer that I went home early because I felt sick. My parents aren't home to miss me, and I can spend the night in the museum."

"What!" Robbie said.

"I'm going to spend the night here. Think of all the things I could do with nobody around watching me." Andrew glanced quickly around the room. Then he walked over to a wall that was covered by long, heavy velvet curtains. He pulled the curtains aside and looked behind them.

"There's enough room for me to hide here," he whispered. "All you have to do is cover for me. You decide right now whether or not you're going to be my friend."

"Okay," Robbie said, "okay."

Andrew took a quick look around the room and then slipped behind the curtains. Robbie walked away to join Mr. Archer and tell him the lie.

Andrew woke up with a sudden start. For a moment, he wasn't sure where he was. Then he remembered . . . the wax museum. He was hiding behind the curtains in the wax museum. He must have fallen asleep earlier in the night because the air was so hot and musty. He pulled back the curtains to peer out.

The museum was empty and closed. Only a few security lights shone on the exhibits. Andrew checked his watch. Two minutes after midnight. He wondered what had woken him at this hour. Just then, he heard a tapping of something against wood. He turned to look at the exhibit where Hitler stood. A feeling of sickening horror swept over him.

Hitler was tapping a wooden map pointer against his desk. He was pointing around the room and talking to his officers. Andrew pinched himself hard to make sure he wasn't having a terrible nightmare. Just then, he saw Hitler's dark, beady eyes meet his. Hitler let out a scream and barked orders at his officers. Andrew watched with terror as they all began to move from the exhibit and climb over the railing into the room.

Andrew scrambled to his feet and ran for the exit. He glanced back to see Hitler's angry face sneering at him. There was a red mark on his white face where Andrew had pulled off part of his mustache.

Andrew raced down the narrow hallway through the other exhibits. His heart was pounding wildly, and his brain was slowly turning panicky. He fumbled in his pocket for the tuft of hair that he had pulled from Hitler's face. When he found it, he threw the hair on the floor and stumbled on.

The pounding of the Germans' feet was loud behind him, but Andrew gained distance on them as he turned a corner in the aisle. Then, in front of him, he saw Napoléon. The emperor slowly drew his hand out of his jacket and reached for his sword. Andrew's stomach turned inside him as Napoléon pulled the sword from its sheath and leaped over the railing.

Andrew remembered the pin he had stuck in the wax figure. Only the figure wasn't wax anymore. Napoléon was alive and breathing minutes, two of the dogs came panting back to the cabin. But no matter how hard Jake called, the third dog never returned from the woods.

Jake bolted the door and went back to bed with the two dogs lying underneath him. Again his stomach rumbled from his strange meal, and the wind whistled around the cabin.

Then Jake heard a scratching noise outside his door. It was the sound of claws scraping against the wood. And the weird voice started up again, "Tailypo, Tailypo, give me back my Tailypo."

Jake shrunk back into the bed and covered his head with a blanket. But the weird voice came even louder. "Tailypo, Tailypo, give me back my Tailypo. You have got it; that I know. Give me back my Tailypo."

The two dogs under the bed were growling, and Jake whistled them out. Again he threw open the door, and the dogs went bounding out after the creature.

With loud screeching and howling, the dogs chased the animal into the woods. Jake waited and listened. Soon he saw just one dog running back to the cabin in the moonlight. The dog whimpered as Jake let it in the door; then it ran under the bed and hid.

Jake bolted the door and crawled in bed. But he hadn't even shut his eyes before he heard the scratching of claws on the door. And the weird voice said, "Tailypo, Tailypo, give me back my Tailypo."

Jake jumped out of bed and whistled for his last dog. It growled from under the bed and wouldn't come out. Finally Jake dragged it out and pulled it to the door. He opened the door and forced the dog out after the creature.

There was a short howl and then a long screech. Jake waited and listened. After ten minutes, he opened the door and called for the dog. But nothing came back out of the dark woods around the cabin.

Jake slammed the door shut quickly, bolted it, and jumped into his bed. He was shivering hard, but the blankets didn't seem to make him warmer. He waited and waited. The wind whistled louder around the cabin. Jake strained his ears to hear the sound of claws scratching on the door. He waited for the weird voice. He heard nothing but the sound of the wind. Jake waited and listened. Then finally he fell asleep.

With a start, Jake woke up. He heard the sound of claws scratching against wood. But this time, the sound was closer and louder.

Jake's eyes flew open and met the burning yellow eyes staring at him from the end of his bed. The creature sat there, scratching its claws against the bedpost.

"Tailypo, Tailypo, give me back my Tailypo," it said in its weird voice.

"I . . . I . . . don't have it," Jake stammered.

The creature crawled forward on the bed. Its face was only a foot from Jake's.

"Tailypo, Tailypo, give me back my Tailypo. You have got it; that I know. Give me back my Tailypo!"

Jake was never seen in the hills again. And the mountain folk say that if you are all alone at night and listen carefully, you can hear a weird voice calling on the wind:

"Tailypo, Tailypo, now I have my Tailypo!"

Words of Warning

Peter had been in Greenfield for only one day when he heard the story. The old man who told it to him had acted strange, but the story was stranger yet. Peter didn't believe in things like ghosts or haunted houses . . . but it gave him the creeps to think about them.

The old man, whose name was Charlie, had warned him not to go near an abandoned house that was nearby. In the past five years, five boys and girls had last been seen walking toward it. They had disappeared into thin air. The only explanation was that the house was possessed by some strange power.

Peter stood on the porch of the country inn where his family was staying, and he wished that he were home. His parents had driven for hours out of the city to spend the autumn weekend here. They had come to see the fall leaves that turned spectacular colors in this remote part of New England.

Peter was already bored by looking at the leaves, and he couldn't get his mind off Charlie's strange story. Charlie was the gardener for the inn. He said that he'd noticed Peter's hair right away when he had arrived at the inn. That had made Peter uncomfortable, because he didn't like people noticing his red hair.

Charlie said he didn't warn every boy or girl who stopped at the inn about the story, but he felt obliged to tell Peter. The owners of the inn refused to talk about the five boys and girls who had disappeared. They worried that it would be bad for business.

Peter decided he couldn't stand around another second. He ran down the steps of the porch and started down the driveway leading away from the inn. He knew his parents wouldn't miss him. They had left the inn an hour ago to take a walk in the woods. They had carried along their binoculars just in case they sighted an interesting bird. Peter had turned down their invitation to join them. He wasn't interested in bird-watching, and he didn't care about the red, orange, and yellow leaves he was kicking as he walked down the lane.

Several yards ahead, Peter saw a fork in the road. The way leading off to the left was the more traveled road that his father had driven down as they came up to the inn. The way to the right narrowed down to a footpath through a thick stand of trees. A slight tingle ran down Peter's spine as he realized his mind was made up. He was going to take the path to the right, the path that led to the old house that Charlie had told him to stay away from.

As Peter walked down the path, he noticed that the leaves covering it looked undisturbed, as if no one had walked there before him. Yet the path was easy to follow as it cut through the trees and thick undergrowth on the forest floor. Peter suddenly got an eerie feeling at the back of his neck and turned quickly around. But the only thing he saw was a pair of red leaves drifting slowly down to the ground.

Peter walked on for fifteen minutes, looking ahead and seeing nothing but more trees. He began to wonder if the old man had played a joke on him, a kid from the city. But then he came to a wide clearing in the trees, and standing there, like a scene from a horror movie, was a gray-shingled, dilapidated house.

A whirlwind of leaves suddenly blew around in front of Peter as a cloud passed over the sun. The colors of the leaves faded without the sunlight, and the house seemed to cast a shadow over everything around it.

Peter pushed back the feeling of panic that had started growing in his mind. He took a few more steps toward the house. It was an old, rambling, three-story structure with a porch all around it. Many of its windows were broken. The porch sagged at a sickening angle, and the shutters hung crookedly on their hinges.

Peter thought about his friends back home. They would love hearing his story about this house. But they would ask if he'd gone inside. And if he said no, they would call him a chicken.

Peter tried not to think too much and began to walk up to the house with quick strides. But the old man's story kept coming back into his mind. The strange story seemed more real now that he was standing in front of the house. He hesitated before setting his foot on the first step of the stairs leading up to the porch.

The wind had died down and there wasn't a sound except the occasional call of a bird in the woods. Peter stood there, undecided. He heard a faint noise inside the house. It grew a little louder, a strange kind of noise he'd never heard before. Then a weird sensation came over him. He felt drawn toward the house as though something were pulling him inside. Unwillingly, his right foot went forward and stepped up onto the first step. Peter screamed and pulled his body back. He scrambled back from whatever power had come over him and ran into the woods. He tore along the path, bumping into trees and scratching himself on branches. Ten minutes later, he ran up to the inn, where his mother and father were sitting on the porch.

"Peter, what happened?" his mother asked.

"Nothing," Peter gasped, his heart pounding in his ears, "just nothing."

The next day, more guests arrived at the inn. Peter sat on the porch and watched them as they unpacked their cars and settled in. One family had two boys near his age. They came out on the porch and introduced themselves right away. Brian, who was tall and skinny and had dark brown hair, was fourteen. Jeff, who was short and stocky and had blond hair, was twelve. Peter noticed the old gardener Charlie staring at them from the yard, but he just kept raking leaves.

"So, what's there to do around here?" Jeff said. "My parents brought us up here to look at leaves. So here are the leaves. What do we do now?"

"There isn't even a television in our room," Brian said. "I can't believe we're stuck here for a whole weekend."

"What have you been doing?" Jeff asked. "Watching birds?"

Peter sat up straight. He could tell them something exciting.

"I went to a haunted house yesterday," he said. "It's not far from here — and it's really creepy."

Jeff let out a high-pitched laugh. "You believe in haunted houses? I can't take it!"

Peter felt a blush creeping over his face. "I'll show you where it is," he said. "You can see for yourself."

"Great, we'll meet you on the front steps in half an hour," Brain said. "Right after we unpack."

"In half an hour," Peter repeated. As they walked away, he looked out at Charlie raking the leaves. He wondered why Charlie hadn't warned Jeff and Brian about the house.

Half an hour later, Peter stood waiting by the front steps of the inn. He kicked a pile of leaves impatiently, wondering if Jeff and Brian would show up. He wished they would hurry. If Charlie happened to come around to the front, Peter didn't want him to see them going off in the direction of the old house.

Finally the screen door of the inn slammed loudly and Jeff and Brian bounded down the steps at a run.

"Lead the way," they yelled to Peter.

The three boys ran off down the land and, at the fork, took the path to the right that led to the old house. Peter was running in the lead, with the two boys close behind him. As the path grew more narrow, they slowed their pace to a walk.

"Were you kidding us about this house?" Jeff asked as they walked through the carpet of leaves that had grown even thicker.

"It's here, all right," Peter said. He knew the house was only a few minutes away, because his chest had started to grow heavy with anxiety.

Soon they walked out into the clearing

around the house. Peter looked at the house, hulking like a dark giant among the brightly colored trees, and shuddered.

"Wow," Jeff whispered. "It looks haunted all right!"

"Let's go," Brian yelled, starting toward the house at a run. Jeff ran quickly after him.

"No, wait!" Peter screamed. He stayed where he was at the edge of the clearing. The other boys turned around and stared at him.

"What's the matter with you?" Jeff asked. "Are you chicken?"

"I wouldn't go any farther if I were you," Peter warned.

The two boys laughed at him and ran up to the house. Peter watched as they bounded up the porch stairs two at a time. Brian reached the door first. He grabbed the old handle and gave it a hard push. The door swung open with a sickening creak.

Peter took a few steps closer to the house. Brian and Jeff looked back at him and laughed again. Then they both went inside the house. Peter felt a sweat break out on his brow. He couldn't bring himself to go up to the house, no matter how he willed his feet to move forward.

Ten minutes later, Brian and Jeff came out

of the house covered with dust and cobwebs.

"Some haunted house," Jeff said. "All that's in there is a bunch of old furniture."

"Why didn't you come in?" Brian asked. "You're not really afraid of that place, are you?"

"Come on, I've got to get back," Peter said, starting off down the path to the inn.

"Chicken," Jeff whispered behind his back.

"Chicken," Brian echoed.

The next day Jeff and Brian ignored Peter. He knew what they thought of him. And he was beginning to think they were right. Why should he be afraid of the old house if the two of them had walked around inside it and not seen or heard a thing? He had just let the old man's story get to his imagination.

Peter nervously ran his hand through his red hair. Then he made up his mind. He was going back to the house. He would prove to himself that he wasn't a chicken. And he would come back and tell Jeff and Brian what he'd done. Maybe he could even bring something back from inside to prove it.

Peter looked up as he set off from the inn. Storm clouds were gathering in the late afternoon sky. A chilling autumn wind cut through his sweater and blew the leaves off the trees in swirling clumps. The path leading to the old house looked different today. Many of the trees along it had been stripped almost bare of their leaves. The white birches looked like skeletons shivering in the wind. Peter stuck his hands in his pockets and kicked fiercely through the leaves at his feet. Why had Charlie ever told him that story anyway?

Peter started to run along the path to warm himself up. The sooner he got to the house, the sooner it would be over. Within a short time, he was standing at the clearing with the house in front of him.

Just like yesterday, he found that his legs were suddenly frozen with fear. The house looked evil today, hunched under the dark gray sky. Peter forced himself to walk toward it. He hugged his arms around his body, trying to keep himself from shaking. Step by step, he drew nearer to the stairs going up to the front porch.

The old man's words of warning went through his mind, but Peter ignored them. He couldn't stop now. A step away from the stairs, he heard the same weird, whooshing noise he'd heard before. A swell of panic rose inside him. He tried to stop his foot from stepping onto the first stair. But it was too late. Just then, two invisible arms grabbed hold of him and pulled him up the stairs onto the porch. And then, in front of him, the door to the house swung open as if pushed by an invisible hand.

Peter felt himself being pulled inside the house. He couldn't run away. He couldn't escape. The door slammed behind him.

Peter looked around the room in terror. Five ghostly faces stared back at him. And finally, Peter understood the old man's words of warning . . . for each ghost had red hair.

The Ghost's Revenge

The young Confederate soldiers marched along the road, their bodies exhausted from battle, their uniforms bloody and torn. But they were the lucky ones. They had survived the awful battle that the Union soldiers had won. Many of their friends lay dead on the battlefield, never to return.

A young lieutenant named William Compton rode his horse alongside them. It had been his first battle, and he had seen things he wanted to forget. Several times, he had smelled death lurking near him, but he had escaped. William looked up from the dusty road to see a carriage passing by the line of soldiers. A pretty young girl sat in it. She met his eyes and smiled.

Inside the carriage, Lucy Potter continued

to smile. The young officer had looked dirty and tired, but he was very handsome. Like many young men, he obviously found her lovely to look at. Lucy had just turned seventeen, and she spent a great deal of time in front of the mirror.

The carriage jolted on down the rough road, carrying Lucy to her uncle's plantation in the country. She had had to flee from the city where she was going to a boarding school when the Union soldiers had drawn too near. Her rich uncle had offered to take her in, since she had been orphaned three years ago when both her parents had died in an epidemic.

Lucy stuck her head out the carriage window to peer back at the soldiers. The war was exciting to her, and she thought the young men looked brave and dashing in their uniforms. Someday soon she hoped to meet a handsome, rich man and marry him.

The shadows of night were falling over the white-columned mansion when Lucy arrived at her uncle's house. It was a beautiful, spacious house — very different from the modest home Lucy had grown up in. As she walked up to the door held open by a servant, she vowed to live this life always. She must simply marry the right husband.

Lucy's aunt and uncle received her with affection and hospitality. She was shown to a beautiful bedroom with a closet full of expensive dresses that had belonged to her cousin Eleanor, who had died in the same epidemic as Lucy's parents. Before she went to bed, Lucy tried many of the dresses on. She looked in the mirror and smiled. Her new life was beginning.

In the middle of that night, a knock sounded on the mansion door. Lucy's uncle, Thomas Potter, opened it and saw an exhausted Confederate captain standing there. The officer asked if his soldiers could spend the night on Mr. Potter's land. Mr. Potter readily agreed and invited the officer and his lieutenants to stay in the mansion.

Lucy came down for breakfast the next morning dressed in a rose-colored silk dress that cast a glow over her white skin and set off her deep blue eyes. She walked into the dining room, expecting to greet only her aunt and uncle. She was startled to see four young men and one older man sitting with her relatives. They were all dressed in the gray uniforms of officers of the Confederate army.

"My niece, Lucy Potter," her uncle said graciously. Then, as all the officers rose to meet her, he introduced each of them. Lucy nodded and smiled to each. But she smiled most when she was introduced to Lieutenant William Compton. She remembered having seen his handsome face from her carriage the day before. Today it was scrubbed clean and his auburn hair shone in the sunlight. She took her place across from his at the long table set with fine china and silver.

During the breakfast, while Mr. Potter and the officers discussed the progress of the war, Lucy often looked up to see William Compton staring at her with a longing look in his brown eyes. She let herself blush, knowing it complimented her.

"I insist that you and your men stay on the plantation until you get further orders," Mr. Potter said to the captain.

"Thank you, sir," the captain answered. "My men need to stop running for a while. The war has taken its toll on them."

Lucy looked again at Lieutenant Compton and saw the happiness on his face. She wondered if he was as rich as he was handsome. She vowed to find out as soon as possible.

That afternoon, from her bedroom window, Lucy saw Lieutenant Compton walking in the rose garden near the mansion. She look a last look in the mirror, then hurried down the wide staircase, out the door of the mansion, and down the path to the rose garden. She slowed down when she saw the lieutenant leaning against an old oak ahead.

"Lucy," he said with more feeling than he wanted to betray when he saw her. "Excuse me, I mean Miss Potter."

She insisted that he call her Lucy, and he asked that she call him William. By the time they had walked around the rose garden twice, she knew that he was in love with her. War had brought his feelings close to the surface and made them intense.

Once he started to tell her about the terrible battle he'd just been in, but then stopped. He turned away and broke off a red rose from a nearby bush. He picked off the thorns and gave it to Lucy with a look that made her heart pound.

That evening they sat beside each other at dinner and shared private conversation while the others talked about Mr. Lincoln and the war. Lucy went to bed that night with her head swimming with thoughts of William. She reminded herself that tomorrow she must find out how rich he was.

The next evening, as they sat together in the rose garden after dinner, Lucy asked William where his home was. But instead of hearing about a white mansion like her uncle's, she heard about a wood-frame house like the one she had grown up in. Her heart sank as she listened to him speak sadly of his widowed mother, living a life made poorer by the war. But his words faded from her mind when he kissed her under a tree in the shadows of the Spanish moss that hung like a canopy around them.

The soldiers stayed on for three more weeks while General Lee planned his next move against the Union army. Lucy and William spent their days together and dreamed of each other at night. Then one morning the captain made an announcement at breakfast.

"Tomorrow we march north," he said. "The Union army is on the move again. We'll meet them in battle fifty miles north of here."

Lucy met William's eyes and saw the shudder pass through his body. The captain gave orders to his lieutenants about all they had to do that day. Before he left, William made Lucy promise to meet him in the rose garden that night.

They met under the same tree as before. Lucy's heart beat fast as she watched William pull out something small and shiny from the pocket of his uniform. Then she felt him slip the smooth, gold band onto the ring finger of her left hand.

"Marry me, Lucy, when I come back," he said, dropping down on one knee as he asked her.

Lucy looked at the plain ring in the moonlight. She had always dreamed of a diamond ring, a huge stone that sent off glints of fire. But then she looked down at William's face. He was going off to battle the next day. She said she would marry him.

William stood up and kissed her. Then he held her shoulders tightly in his hands and stared intently into her eyes. "Promise me something, Lucy," he asked. "If I don't come back from this battle, say you'll never marry anyone else."

Lucy hesitated. She twisted the tight ring

around her finger. William was still staring into her eyes. "I promise, William. I'll never marry anyone but you."

The soldiers left the next morning. William rode away on his horse, waving good-bye to Lucy on the steps of the mansion. Lucy nervously twisted the ring on her finger as she watched him until he rode out of sight. Then she went up to her room and stared in the mirror.

Five nights later, there was another knock on the mansion door. Again Mr. Potter opened it to find an exhausted Confederate officer. He was a young captain with news of the terrible battle that had taken place fifty miles to the north. The South had lost the battle and suffered a great loss of men. Captain Sanders asked if he and his men could stay on Mr. Potter's land. Before he left to settle in his men, he gave one more piece of news. Another captain had told him to bring news about Lieutenant William Compton to Miss Lucy Potter. Lieutenant Compton had been shot in the battle and was dead.

When Mr. Potter broke the news to Lucy the next morning, he waited for her to cry. But she seemed to take William's death with great calm. She only betrayed her feelings by twisting the gold ring around her finger over and over again.

The next weeks were confused and chaotic in the mansion. The young captain had moved into the house with his other officers. The servants and family tended to the sick and wounded soldiers quartered in the barns. Lucy found that the memories of William that haunted her were eased by the presence of Captain Sanders. She found him handsome and was fascinated by the stories he told of his father's plantation, which was still prosperous and safe in the Deep South. Lucy suspected that Captain Sanders found her attractive, but he was too much of a gentleman to show it, especially since he had brought the news of her fiance's death.

One day Captain Sanders offered to take her to the cemetery where the Confederate soldiers killed in the great battle had been buried. Lieutenant Compton was among them. Lucy eagerly accepted his invitation, and when the day came, she chose to wear a brightly colored dress that complimented her. She rode in the carriage with the captain to the cemetery, nervously twisting the gold band around her finger as she listened to his stories of his life before the war.

When the captain took her to William's grave, she insisted that she be left alone there. And when she saw that Captain Sanders was out of sight, she pulled the gold ring off her finger and threw it among the weeds that had already sprung up over William's grave.

Her aunt and uncle were shocked when, two months later, Captain Sanders announced that Lucy had agreed to marry him. They were both eager to be married before the next great battle. Hastily, Mr. Potter arranged for the wedding to take place the next Saturday in the local church.

Lucy walked around the mansion as if on air, showing everyone the beautiful diamond engagement ring that Captain Sanders had given her. The best seamstress in the county was hired to work day and night to make a beautiful silk and lace wedding gown. Only once did her aunt dare to mention William Compton's name. Lucy had screamed that she never wanted to hear of him again, and she had twisted the diamond ring on her finger so hard that she cut herself.

On the morning of her wedding, Lucy walked down the aisle of the small country church on the arm of her uncle. She stared lovingly into the eyes of her bridegroom as he waited for her at the altar.

The minister began the ceremony. As she came closer and closer to the moment when she would become Captain Sander's rich and beautiful wife, Lucy felt a nervousness rising inside her. The ring on her finger seemed to be burning with unnatural heat, and Lucy had to hold herself back from twisting it around and around.

The minister came to the familiar words of the wedding ceremony, just before he pronounced them man and wife. "If anyone has cause to stop this marriage, let him speak now . . . or forever hold his peace."

Lucy felt a horrible coldness start at the back of her neck and then creep all through her body. Then she heard the bang of a door and felt a cold wind rush up the aisle. Like everyone else in the church, she turned around. She met the gaze of William Compton, standing at the back of the church.

As he walked, step by step, up the aisle toward her, Lucy saw the red stain on his gray uniform. It looked like a red rose over his heart. But as he came closer and closer, she saw that it was blood.

William's eyes burned like fire, but his face was the horrible white of death. Lucy shrank back and clasped her right hand over the diamond ring to hide it. Everyone else seemed frozen by the cold, cold wind that blew through the church like a whirlwind with William at its center.

Lucy screamed in horror as she saw William's white, bony hands reach out toward her. Then she felt herself being swooped up in a deathly grip and carried down the aisle by her ghostly bridegroom.

When Captain Sanders and Lucy's relatives rushed out of the church, they could find no sign of Lucy. They only heard the eerie clip-clopping of a horse's hoofs breaking into a gallop.

The men called for their horses and rode off in the direction of the sound the horse had taken. They galloped down the road that led inevitably to the graveyard where William

Compton had been laid to his uneasy rest. Captain Sanders ran through the tombstones to the place where he had brought Lucy only a short time before.

The weeds had grown higher on the grave. Lucy lay dead among them, her hands clutching the tombstone. And on the third finger of her left hand was the plain gold ring . . . that William Compton had given his bride.

A Special Treat

It was exactly one year since Lisa and Harry had been married. For their first anniversary, Lisa prepared a meal that she knew Harry would love. As she stood in the kitchen, ready to serve the first course, Lisa ran through the menu in her mind. Cream of broccoli soup. Stuffed mushrooms. Baked trout Florentine. Potatoes au gratin. Tossed salad. Chocolate mousse.

Then Lisa sighed. Of course, there was no red meat. Red meat was not allowed.

Harry's face broke into a smile as Lisa brought in the soup. They sat down, wished each other a happy anniversary, and began to eat. Lisa watched her husband with adoring eyes. She thought he was very handsome, even though her parents thought he should trim his full beard and thick hair.

As they ate one course after another, Harry complimented Lisa on each dish. He finished off the dessert of chocolate mousse with a satisfied sigh. "I'm the luckiest man in the world," he said, smiling at Lisa. "You're a wonderful cook."

"Thank you," Lisa said. Then she quickly added, "Perhaps I could make you a steak, or even just a hamburger, some night."

"Lisa," Harry said sternly. "You know I cannot eat red meat."

"But Harry . . ." Lisa began weakly. She knew it was going to be a hopeless argument.

"My mother said I should never eat red meat," Harry said firmly. "You know that, Lisa. We needn't discuss it further." He got up from his chair and began to clear the table.

"Why should you still do what your mother told you, Harry? You haven't seen her for twenty years."

"During the five years that my mother was at home, I never ate red meat," Harry replied. "And the last words my mother said to me — just as she was running wildly out the door — were: 'Never eat red meat!' "

Lisa decided to drop the subject. After all, it was their anniversary.

But during the next week, Lisa found herself dwelling on Harry's stubbornness each time she cooked a meal. She liked red meat. It wasn't fair to her that she could never enjoy pot roast or leg of lamb or pork chops. Resentment against Harry's mother seethed and grew inside her. His mother must have been crazy, Lisa thought, to run out on Harry and her husband and never come back.

Harry didn't like to talk about his mother, but Lisa brought up the subject one night over a dinner of eggplant lasagna, a meatless dish that Harry loved.

"What sort of food did your mother cook for you, Harry?" Lisa asked calmly.

Harry looked up from his food with a surprised expression on his face. "You know I don't like thinking about my mother, Lisa," he said. "But now that you've brought it up, she made tuna noodle casserole."

"What else?" Lisa asked.

"That's all I remember, tuna noodle casserole," Harry said defensively. "Now can we drop the subject, please."

From that night on, a plan began to form in

Lisa's mind. She would help Harry get over his irrational fear of red meat. His mother had obviously been neurotic, and she had passed on her ridiculous ideas to her son.

Lisa began to study her cookbooks. She needed to find a recipe that changed the texture and appearance of red meat enough to fool Harry. Finally she found something called Noodle Surprise. The main ingredient was noodles in a thick cream sauce spiced with paprika. But hidden in the cream sauce was finely chopped red meat. Lisa put a piece of paper in the book to mark the place. And then she smiled, trying to imagine Harry's surprise when he found out what he had eaten in Noodle Surprise.

Lisa had to wait another week until the right day came for her experiment. One day Harry announced that he would have to work longer than usual the next evening, but he would be home in time for a late dinner. Lisa assured him with a smile that his meal would be waiting when he got home.

The next afternoon, Lisa went to the supermarket and ran up to the meat counter. "One pound of your best beef for roasting," she told the butcher.

She watched as the butcher reached for a

tray of red meat in the display case. Lisa had never seen such red meat. The butcher cut off a large piece, weighed it, and wrapped it up. Lisa gently put it into her shopping cart as though it were precious caviar.

Late that afternoon, she roasted the meat until it was tenderly done. Then she chopped it into fine pieces, stirred it into the cream sauce for Noodle Surprise, and put the dish in the oven to bake. She was just pulling the casserole out of the oven when she felt a kiss on the back of her neck.

Lisa screamed and almost dropped the food. She whirled around to see Harry smiling at her.

"It's only me," he said and then stared at the expression on her face. "Why do you look guilty?"

"Guilty?" Lisa said, setting down the Noodle Surprise. "Don't be silly. I was just hoping to have dinner on the table when you came home."

"What did you make?" Harry asked.

"A special treat," Lisa answered.

She brought the casserole of Noodle Surprise into the dining room and set it down in the middle of the table.

"Lisa, your hands are shaking," Harry said

as she spooned a large serving on his plate. "Did you have a hard day?"

"Not really," Lisa said, putting some Noodle Surprise on her plate. "How was your day?"

She asked Harry question after question to keep him from looking too closely at the food on his plate. Finally he took his first bite. Lisa held her breath as she watched him chew and swallow it.

"Lisa," he asked. "What's that strange taste in this food?"

Lisa's heart began to pound. "Paprika," she answered.

"No, it's not the paprika," Harry said. "It's something else. I've never tasted it before." Harry took another forkful of the casserole and hungrily ate it. "Delicious!" he said with his mouth full.

Lisa had to hide her smile behind her napkin as she watched Harry wolf down the food. She had never seen him eat so greedily.

"More!" Harry demanded, pushing his plate out to her.

"Harry, remember your manners," Lisa said, putting another huge serving on his plate.

A strange sound came from low in Harry's

throat as he began to eat the second helping. Lisa looked up in alarm.

"Harry, did your stomach just growl?" she asked.

Harry didn't answer. He finished the last forkful of food on his plate and pushed it across the table toward her.

"More," he said again, but his voice sounded so strange that Lisa hardly recognized it.

"Harry, really, I don't know what's come over you," Lisa said nervously, serving him more Noodle Surprise.

"I . . . love . . . this . . . food," Harry said in the strange voice. Then he reached his hand out to pull back his plate.

Lisa screamed. Harry's hand was covered with tufts of hair that looked just like his beard. She looked up at his face and saw a strange gleam in his eyes. Harry smiled at her, showing long, pointed teeth.

Lisa screamed again and tried to tug the plate of food away from Harry. He pulled it back away from her.

"No, Harry, no! Don't eat it," she pleaded. "It's red meat!"

For a second, they both froze and stared at each other across the table. Then the doorbell rang. A weird expression came over Harry's face, and he jumped up from the table. Lisa rushed after him to the front door. Then she screamed as Harry flung the door open.

A creature stood there smiling at Harry. She had graying hair all over her body.

"Mother!" Harry growled.

"Harry," the werewolf growled back.

Then, together, they ran wildly out into the night.

Lisa stood in the doorway, staring up at the full moon in the dark sky. She heard the sound of two howls echoing together through the night. Then she walked back into the dining room and sat down, alone.

She knew she would never see Harry again. And she knew that she would never, ever eat red meat.

The Magic Vanishing Box

Ben had wandered into a part of the city that he'd never seen before. The streets were lined with antique shops and second-hand stores. As he passed by one old shop, Ben stopped to look at a display in its window. Sitting in the midst of other antiques was a tattered, black top hat with an old stuffed rabbit popping out of it.

Ben wondered if it was a real magician's hat. Magic was his hobby. It was almost an obsession with him, in fact. He read everything he could about it and practiced tricks in his spare time.

Ben went to the shop door and read the sign: Curiosities of the Past. He pushed open the door and went inside. One glance around the small one-room shop told him it lived up to its name. There were stuffed monkeys sitting beside huge brass candlesticks. There were lifesize china dogs sitting on carved wooden boxes that looked like coffins. The shop was very curious, indeed.

Ben began to look through the knicknacks and larger items displayed on the tables and shelves in the room.

"May I help you?"

Ben whirled around at the sound of the voice. He saw a stooped old man looking at him with piercing eyes.

"I . . . I was just looking around," Ben stammered.

"Take your time, take your time," the man said. "I'll be in the back if you need me. Ring this bell if you want to buy anything." The man gestured to an old brass bell by the cash register and then hobbled off into the back of the store.

Ben shrugged his shoulders and continued to walk around the store. He took a closer look at the silk top hat in the window. It was a magician's hat, but he had no need for another one. Ben wondered if there might be other magic tricks in the store, old ones that he'd never seen before.

For half an hour Ben lost track of the time as he searched through the jumble of odds and ends on display. Then something caught his eye. It was a shiny, black wood box about two feet square. Ben ran his hand over the smooth wood, the brass hinge at the front, and the brass-covered corners.

But what interested him most was the little brass plate on top of the box. It was engraved with the words: *The Magic Vanishing Box*. With care, Ben unlatched the brass hinge at the front of the box and lifted the lid. Inside, there was nothing, just the empty interior of the black wood. Then Ben caught sight of another brass plate on the inside of the lid. It, too, was engraved with words: *Don't catch your hand inside this lid, or else you'll be sorry that you did.*

Ben carefully shut the lid on the box and stared at it for a long time. What was a magic vanishing box? It was probably some sort of joke. Still, Ben wanted it more than he'd wanted anything for a long time. He reached in his pocket to check the money he'd brought along for his trip into the city. Fifteen dollars. And he needed two dollars of that to get home.

All he had to spend on the box was thirteen dollars.

Ben picked up the box and carried it over to the counter by the cash register. He pressed his hand down on the bell. A shrill ding echoed through the store. Soon the old man came out from the back room. He looked at Ben; then he looked at the box. Slowly a strange smile spread over his face.

An hour later, Ben was in his bedroom unwrapping the newspaper that the old man had bundled around the box. His hands were trembling as he set the shiny box on top of his desk. Again he read the words on the brass plate: *The Magic Vanishing Box.* Ben decided he couldn't wait any longer. He had to find out if he had spent his thirteen dollars foolishly. Carefully he opened the lid to the box and looked inside. There were no instructions except for the warning he'd read before: *Don't catch your hand inside this lid, or else you'll be sorry that you did.*

Ben gingerly opened the lid all the way and then looked around the room. What could he experiment with first? His eyes fell on the blue dictionary that sat on his desk. It would just fit into the box, and he wouldn't care in the least if it vanished.

Ben picked up the heavy book and set it into the bottom of the box. Then he cautiously closed the lid by holding on to its front brass hinge. He felt silly about taking the warning inside the box seriously. After all, it was probably just a practical joke. He snapped down the hinge into place and stood staring at the box. There were no magic words to say; no magic wand to wave. Ben waited for a few minutes, then he opened the lid.

The inside of the box was empty.

Ben stared at the empty, black space for a moment, then he picked up the box to look under it. Nothing was there. Carefully, he shut the lid and turned the box over and over, looking for the secret to its magic. He knew there must be a trick. Things didn't just vanish.

At last he found what he was looking for. On one side of the box, right beside the brass corner decoration, was a small brass latch. Ben pulled it until it sprung; then a tiny drawer shot open from the side of the box.

Ben stared down at the weird things inside

the drawer. There was a tiny blue book lying beside a small, life-like figure of a boy. Ben picked up the book first. He squinted to read the small print of the title. It was a dictionary, a perfect miniature version of his dictionary. He flipped through the pages, and then suddenly let it drop as though it had burned him. How had the box done that? What kind of magic did it have?

Ben's eyes were drawn to the small figure of the boy. It was only about two inches high and was dressed in old-fashioned clothes. The details of its face and clothing were so realistic that it could have been alive, except that it was so small.

Ben set the tiny book and the figure on his bookshelf. Then he shut the secret drawer, opened the box lid, and looked around his room for something else to test. He still couldn't believe this was happening to him.

He caught sight of his face in the mirror above his dresser. The freckles on his face were standing out against his white skin. He pinched his arm under his red football jersey, just to make sure he was awake. The box was the strangest trick he had ever used. And there was something even more strange. It didn't seem to be just a trick — it was real magic.

Ben picked up a pencil, put it in the box, and shut the lid. A minute later, he pushed the latch on the secret drawer. It shot open, and inside was a perfect replica of the pencil, so little that Ben could hardly pick it up.

Ben looked at the clock in his room. He knew his parents would be home soon, and he wanted to keep the box a secret. But he had to try the trick just one more time. This time he would put in something unusual. He looked up and saw his transistor radio. Would the radio still be able to play music if it were turned into a miniature?

Ben opened the lid of the box and reached up for his radio. It just fit inside the box. As he started to close the lid, Ben saw that the radio's antenna was sticking up. He reached one hand inside the box to push the antenna down.

Just then his mother's voice called from downstairs, "Ben, we're home."

Ben swung his head around in panic. Then the heavy, black lid of the box slammed down on his hand. For a second it hurt. Then Ben felt nothing.

* * *

For a year the police searched for Ben. But the only clues they had to work with were the strange black box and the tiny book and figure they found in his room. Finally the police gave up. Ben's parents cleaned out his room and gave away his belongings. And eventually the black box made its way back to the old antique shop where Ben had bought it.

The old man sat it back on its shelf. It waited there for another boy to come in and buy it. And that boy would find its secret drawer — and, inside the drawer, a small life-like figure of a boy with freckles wearing a red football jersey.

Wait Till Max Comes

One dark and stormy night, a stranger walked down a lonely road between two villages. He had traveled for several miles without seeing a house, and he was growing more and more worried about the weather.

A cold wind had sprung up, whipping the tree branches around and blowing dust into his eyes. The sky was dark with angry thunder-clouds, even though sunset was still an hour away. Then a streak of lightning cut through the black clouds, making everything suddenly bright. It was followed by a rumble of thunder that rocked the earth.

The man stopped in his tracks and began to tremble. There was going to be a terrible storm. He had to find shelter.

He peered through the trees that lined both sides of the road, but the light had grown so dim that he could see nothing but shadows. Then another jagged bolt of lightning shot through the sky. The man looked up and saw the silhouette of a house against the sky. It sat on top of a hill above the road.

The man waited, and another flash of lightning came. By its light he saw the entrance to a narrow lane along the road. He stumbled over to it and started to climb the winding path up to the house.

Hard drops of rain splattered down on the man's bare head. The ground beneath his feet became slippery as it grew wetter and wetter. By now the man was panting from trying to run up the hill. He began to doubt whether this lane led to the house at all.

Then suddenly he walked out of the narrow lane and into a clearing. A streak of lightning shot across the sky and lit up a huge house with pointed gables and dark windows that looked like sinister eyes. The man drew back and gasped. The house looked like an evil animal, crouched in the dark. He thought about running back down the lane to the road.

But then the wind sprang up even harder,

whipping the cold rain against the man's body. He ran for the house and found the front door. To his surprise, the latch opened when he tried it. Cautiously he crept inside and shut the door behind him.

The house was as still as a tomb. The man could hear the pounding of the rain outside, but inside all was silent. He fumbled in his pocket and found a match. He struck it, and the burst of flame lit up the hallway he stood in. A pair of candlesticks sat on the table nearby. He lit a candle, picked it up, and began to walk through the house.

The first room he stepped into had a big fireplace with wood stacked in it. The man bent down and lit the wood with his candle flame. Before long, the room was filled with the warm crackle of a burning fire. The man could see the broken-out glass in several of the windows and the thick layer of dust that covered everything in the room.

He sat down in the chair that was pulled up by the fireplace and warmed his cold, weary body. Perhaps he was safe here after all, he thought.

The man had just shut his eyes to sleep when he heard a soft, little cry. He opened his eyes and saw a small, gray kitten sitting on the hearth by the fire. It looked up at him and meowed again.

The kitten made the man feel even more peaceful and secure. Once again, he shut his eyes. Then he heard another cry. This time it was louder and stronger. He opened his eyes and saw a full-grown, striped cat sitting beside the little, gray kitten. Now four green eyes stared back at him from the hearthside.

The man liked cats, so this did not bother him very much. Once again, he shut his eyes.

"What will we do with him?"

The man's eyes flew open. Who had said that? He searched around the room. But he saw only the two cats sitting by the fireplace. It must have been his imagination, he told himself.

Then he saw the striped cat turn to the gray kitten and say, "Wait till Max comes."

The man started to tremble and squeezed his eyes shut. Maybe he was losing his mind. Then he heard another sound, a very loud hiss.

He looked at the hearth and saw a third cat, yellow and as big as a dog, sitting beside the other two.

"What'll we do with him?" the striped cat asked.

"Wait till Max comes," the yellow cat said.

The man began to wonder how fast he could run for the door. But it was too late. Just then, a fourth cat walked into the room. It was as big as a leopard and as black as the night. Its eyes were yellow instead of green and they looked the man over from head to toe.

"What should we do with him?" the yellow cat asked.

"Wait till Max comes," the black cat said. Then it sat down in front of the doorway.

The man looked at the four cats staring at him hungrily. Then he looked over at the window nearest him that had its glass broken out. With one leap, the man sprang from the chair and jumped out the window.

"Tell Max I couldn't wait!" he screamed.

The man ran home, locked himself in his house, and never came out again. For he knew that somewhere, out there, Max was waiting for him.

The Old Beggar Woman

It was a time of hardship and poverty in the villages along the New England coast. The crops had failed, and food was scarce. Beggars, wearing tattered clothes and haunting faces, roamed the countryside asking for food or shelter for the night. Good people shared the little they had with the starving poor. But one person turned away from them and admired her plump image in the mirror.

Mrs. Agatha Parry lived in a splendid mansion on top of a high cliff overlooking the Atlantic Ocean. Her husband had owned a whole fleet of whaling ships and had become rich from the profits of whale oil. Captain Parry had died five years earlier, leaving his widow the richest woman in the county.

Some people said that Agatha Parry had become mean and stingy after her husband's death. Others said she had always been so; her husband had made up for it by his generosity to the poor and unfortunate. Stories and rumors flew around the nearby towns about Agatha Parry. She had nearly starved a maid to death for not polishing the silver well enough. She insisted that leftover food be fed to her lap dogs rather than given to the poor. She wouldn't let beggars come to the mansion doors and made her servants push them away into the dark and cold night.

Agatha Parry seldom went to town. She had everything on her estate that she could wish for. Her mansion was filled with paintings by famous artists. There was a music room with a grand piano and a gold harp. In the dining room Agatha Parry ate at the head of a long table laid with fine china and silver. Her guests, mostly wealthy people from far away, were still not as wealthy as she and greedily ate the delicacies set before them.

If it were not for her daily walk along the cliffs, Agatha Parry would never have seen the poor and starving people who lived around her. But she believed that the sea air was good for her complexion, so she took a walk in the early evening each day. The beggars had become desperate enough to follow the rich lady to the cliffs and beg for food from her there.

After seeing their hollow faces and dirty clothes, Agatha had held her handkerchief to her nose and screamed for her servants. She demanded that the cliffs be cleared of beggars before her walk from then on. She wouldn't have the sight of these horrid people spoiling her complexion.

One evening, as usual, Agatha set off from her mansion for her walk on the cliffs. The silk skirts of her expensive dress rustled around her. The rings she loved to wear hung heavy on her fingers. By her side walked one of the little lap dogs she loved and pampered.

Her servants had gone back to the mansion after assuring her that the cliffs were empty of beggars. Agatha strolled along the stone cliffs, worn smooth by years of crashing waves. Ahead of her, a large rock jutted into the path. To pass by it, she had to walk close to the edge of the cliff. Her tiny dog began to whimper and wouldn't go further. Agatha snapped her fingers at him angrily, but the dog cowered on the ground. Finally, she bent down and picked him up, and then stepped cautiously around the rock onto the narrow path.

Below, the sea was surging and foaming with the tide. The water looked dark and angry with the sunlight fading in the sky. Agatha had almost walked around the rock when she looked up from the ocean and saw an old woman sitting on a ledge in the rock. With a scream Agatha dropped her little dog. It scampered to safety away from the cliff edge.

"Some food for the starving," the old woman begged in a cracked voice.

Agatha looked at the beggar with disgust. The woman was dressed in black rags with an old black cape thrown around her shoulders. Her yellowed teeth were long and pointed. Her dark eyes seemed to glow in her old, wrinkled face. And her gnarled fingers shook as they reached out to Agatha, pleading.

"Go away, old woman," Agatha said. She wanted to run away herself, but her legs had become weak with fright.

"Rich lady, I am starving," the old woman said. "Give me just one coin to buy food with."

"Leave me alone," Agatha screamed. But still she couldn't run away from the woman. Their eyes met, and Agatha felt fear creep through her veins like a bitter poison.

"If you do not give me something to eat, I will die," the old beggar woman said in a shaking voice. "And someday, you will be like me, poor and ugly and starving."

Agatha twisted her eyes away from the woman's gaze. "I'll never be like you," she hissed. Then she looked down at the rings on her hands and pulled from one finger a gold ring engraved with her initials.

"I can never be poor," she said, "just as this ring can never return from the sea." Then she threw the ring over the cliff into the roaring ocean.

The old woman muttered strange words and looked out to the sea. Agatha suddenly found her strength and ran back along the cliff path to her mansion.

That night Agatha did not enjoy the delicious meal set before her on the long table. The roast beef tasted dry in her mouth, even though it had been cooked to perfection. The rich chocolate dessert seemed bitter rather than sweet, and Agatha pushed it away uneaten. She walked to the fireplace and sat down in a chair in front of it. But when she stared into the flames, she seemed to see the old woman's eyes glowing back at her.

The next evening she began to take her walk on the cliffs again. But a servant hurried to stop her. He said he had found a dead body on a rock ledge and had called the villagers to take it away. Mrs. Parry would have to wait until the woman was removed.

Agatha hurried back into her mansion. She didn't have to ask what the woman looked like. She knew exactly how the old, wrinkled face would look in death.

That night was Agatha's first of many sleepless nights. She put on her lace and silk nightgown, lay her head down on the goose-feather pillows, shut her eyes, and saw the old woman's glowing eyes, yellow teeth, and gnarled fingers.

A year passed. Agatha's once plump figure had become thin and bony, and her rich clothes hung loose on her. She no longer took walks along the cliffs, and her complexion had grown dry and wrinkled. Doctors were called to help her sleep and eat, but they did no good.

Agatha became greedier and greedier as she became thinner and thinner. During the nights when she couldn't sleep, she counted her money or rearranged her jewels in her drawers. Often she thought of the gold ring she had thrown into the sea.

One night she decided she would have a grand dinner and invite all her rich friends whom she hadn't seen for over a year. She must let them know that she was still rich and well, just in case they had heard rumors to the opposite. She sent her servants to buy the most expensive foods and wines for the dinner. She ordered delicacies from all over the world. No expense was spared to get the mansion ready.

At last the night of the great dinner arrived. Agatha's old friends poured into the house, curious and eager to see her. She noticed the surprise on their faces when she greeted them. With artificial smiles, they told her how well she looked.

Agatha led them into the dining room, where the long table was set with sparkling silver and shining china. She took her place at the head of the table and gestured to the servants to begin serving. The guests ate their first, second, and third courses while Agatha watched. She left the food put on her plate untouched, for she had no appetite.

Then a servant came in carrying a large,

domed platter. He set it on the table in front of Agatha and, with a flourish, whisked off the top. Under the dome was a huge whole fish. The guests let out a murmur of amazement.

The servant picked up a knife and began to carve the fish. He cut down its long body and then opened it up. Suddenly, with a loud clatter, he dropped the knife on the silver plate. Agatha looked up at the servant with irritation, then she followed his eyes down to the platter.

There, inside the fish's belly, was a gold ring, shining in the candlelight. The servant picked it up and handed it to Agatha. With trembling fingers, she turned it around and around until she saw her initials etched in the gold. She remembered the words she had spoken when she threw the ring in the sea. Then, as her guests watched with curious eyes, Agatha jumped up and ran from the table, choking back the scream that was rising in her throat.

That night a fire burned Agatha's house to the ground, destroying all her riches. Agatha escaped with just the clothes she had on and a tattered black cape that a servant had put around her. At daybreak, Agatha stood watching the last embers of her house burn out. Then she pulled the cape closer around her and walked toward the cliffs overlooking the ocean.

And to this day, if you go to a certain place along the cliffs of New England, you might see the ghost of an old beggar woman. And you'll know who she is by the tattered black cape and the gold ring that she still wears.

The Masked Ball

It was Halloween night. A full moon shone down on the mansion where a large party of people danced and laughed at the masked ball. But upstairs in the mansion, one person was not dancing or laughing.

A young woman named Kate was standing alone in a small room. Holding her silvery mask in shaking hands, she stared at her face in a large gilt-framed mirror. Signs of fear and sleeplessness marked her blue eyes. Quickly she slipped the mask back over her face and turned to the door. She would have to go back to the ball . . . even though, somewhere in the crowd, the vampire waited for her.

Out in the corridor, Kate passed a man in a Roman toga and a woman dressed as Cleopatra. Like Kate, they wore masks over their faces. But even without their masks, Kate wouldn't have known them. She only knew the host of the party, an old acquaintance of her father's.

Kate came to the top of the wide, spiral staircase that wound down to the front hallway of the mansion. From below, the sound of laughing and talking floated up to her. Kate put on an artificial smile and, step by step, started down the staircase.

Halfway down, her eyes were caught by a dark figure gliding through the crowd. His black cape swirled as he moved through the brightly colored costumes. Kate's heart skipped a beat, and her knees turned to sand. It was the same man she had glimpsed earlier and run away from. She had only seen his black clothes and his dark, shiny hair. But she knew who he was — the vampire.

Kate forced herself to take another step down the stairs. Then the man turned around and looked up, staring straight at her. In one terrible second, Kate saw the two fangs curving over his red lips. She felt the strength in her legs ebb away. Then her mind went black. . . .

When she opened her eyes, the blackness had gone. Kate looked up into the masked face of a young man with blond hair.

"Are you all right?" he asked.

Kate stood up straight on the staircase and remembered where she was. Many of the masked faces in the hallway below were turned toward her. But the dark figure with the horrible fangs was nowhere to be seen.

"Let me help you down the stairs," the young man said.

Kate turned to him and smiled. He was dressed in a red braided jacket and black pants. A full mask covered his face.

"Thank you," she said. "I must have started to faint."

"Come with me," the young man said. "Perhaps you need something to eat. My name, by the way, is Robert."

"I'm Kate," she answered, feeling as though a shadow had been lifted from the evening.

She walked beside the young man through the crowd of curious masks staring at her. They made their way to the ballroom, where a large table was filled with food. Kate tried to eat a small sandwich but found that her appetite had disappeared.

"I made a fool of myself on the staircase," she said, turning to Robert. "You see, I thought I saw a vampire." She paused and then said, "For many nights now, I have had terrible dreams — nightmares — about a vampire."

Robert stopped eating and stared at her intently. "What are your dreams like?" he asked.

Kate hesitated. She didn't know how her strange story would sound to him. But he waited for her to begin.

"I dream that a vampire dressed all in black is coming to get me," she said. "No matter how I try to escape him, he is always there. And just as I see his fangs, I scream . . . and wake up."

As Kate finished her story, she noticed a change in Robert's eyes. They became harder and darker. Suddenly, she was embarrassed. Perhaps he thought she was crazy.

"I'm sorry," she said. "I'm spoiling your evening. Could we dance?"

Robert took her hand and led her to the dance floor. Soon Kate forgot about the man in black and her nightmare. Then, as another dance began, Kate saw a white hand reach up to Robert's shoulder and tap it. They both turned to face the dark figure standing beside them.

"May I cut in and have this dance with the young lady?" he asked.

Kate shrank back in terror. It was the man in black — the vampire — standing only inches away from her. Her eyes were drawn to his mouth. Now she could see that the fangs were made of plastic and not real at all. But she turned away quickly and gripped Robert's hand tightly in hers.

"I'm sorry," Robert said firmly, "but she wants to stay with me."

Kate watched the black figure slip away like a cat through the crowd.

"That was him, the man I saw before," Kate said as they began to dance again. "Did you see his fangs?"

"They weren't real fangs at all," Robert said. "You shouldn't be afraid of him."

"But I am afraid," Kate said. "My dreams are so real that I'm afraid they might come true."

You are overexcited," Robert said. "It is Halloween night."

His voice sounded hard and cold to Kate, so cold that a chill ran down her spine. Perhaps he was becoming bored by her talk of the vampire. Suddenly Kate wanted to leave the ballroom and breathe fresh air.

"Please come out onto the patio with me," she said. "I can't stand it in here anymore."

Robert led her from the dance floor to a set of French doors that opened up onto the patio. They walked into the warm night air. Kate looked up at the moon in the sky. It still shone brightly, but the shadow of a cloud bank loomed near it.

"Now I feel safe," she said, turning around to look back at the windows of the ballroom. Then she saw the silhouette against the window. It was the vampire, staring out at her on the patio.

Kate choked back a scream and ran down a flight of steps into the garden, pulling Robert along with her.

"It's hard to see," she gasped as they followed a path that twisted among high bushes. "I have to take off my mask." She pulled the silvery mask away from her face and looked at Robert, expecting him to take off his mask as well. But he just stared at her and then hurried down the path.

Suddenly the path ended at the edge of a lake. Kate found herself standing on a narrow wooden dock that had a rowboat tied to it. Robert gestured toward the boat.

"I'll take you for a ride in the moonlight," he said.

Kate stepped into the rowboat. Then, before he got in, Robert unbuttoned his red braid jacket and pulled it off. Kate noticed that now he was dressed all in black. He stepped into the boat, picked up the oars, and pulled the boat away from the dock.

Kate sat up straight in the boat and nervously looked back at the distant lights of the mansion. In front of her, Robert lifted the heavy oars in and out of the water.

"This is hard work," he said. "Would you hold the oars while I take off my wig?"

Kate grasped the oars with both hands and watched with curiosity as he pulled off the blond wig, holding his mask carefully in place with his other hand. As he took the oars back,

Kate noticed how the moonlight shimmered on his shiny black hair.

"Why don't you take off your mask?" Kate asked. "It must be very uncomfortable."

Robert didn't answer, but kept rowing farther and farther away from the shore.

Kate looked up at the moon. It was still shining bright and full, but she could see the corner of the cloud bank drawing nearer to it in the sky. She turned back to look at Robert. His mask looked eerie in the moonlight against the darkness of his hair and clothing.

"Please, take off that mask," Kate asked him.

"When we get to the middle of the lake," he answered. "It will only be a few more minutes."

Kate realized that her heart had begun to pound. She looked wildly around the dark lake, searching for the shoreline. Just then, the clouds passed over the moon. She could only see the shadowy figure in front of her.

Suddenly the sound of the oars lapping in the water stopped. Kate heard them being dragged into the boat. Then all was quiet.

Kate sat very still in the boat as the cold fingers of fear reached around her heart. In the pale light, she could see Robert's hand moving up to take off the mask. Then the moon broke out of the clouds, and a scream rose from deep in Kate's throat.

The light of the moon shone down on the face of the vampire . . . and glittered on his long white fangs.

Skin-and-Bones

It was one hundred years ago, on an autumn night, that Jacob Cooper drew his horse and buggy up to the old inn at twilight. As Jacob tied his horse to the hitching post by the side of the inn, he turned back to look at the western sky. It was purplish red from the setting sun and splotched with angry black clouds. A sharp wind had sprung up and was cutting through Jacob's coat and chilling him to the bone.

Jacob hurried toward the door with a sign hanging over it that read: The Red Fox Inn. As he pushed the door open, he felt a rush of warm air and the smell of cooked food. Jacob walked in, meeting the stares of the three men who sat at a table eating and drinking. A red-cheeked man stood behind the bar, polishing its shiny mahogany surface.

"Evening," Jacob said, sitting down at a table. "I'd like some hot roast beef and whatever you have to go with it," he said to the man behind the bar.

"You look half frozen," the man said in a friendly way as he turned to go into the kitchen to get Jacob's food.

"Cold out there?" one of the men at the table said.

Jacob nodded his head and rubbed his hands together.

"Good thing you're at a warm, safe inn," another man said. "I wouldn't want to travel hereabouts on such a night."

"I just stopped for food," Jacob explained as the rosy-cheeked man brought out his food from the kitchen. "I have to travel ten miles yet tonight. My friend in Platkill is expecting me."

Jacob noticed that the four men had fallen silent and were looking at each other uneasily.

"You'd better tell him, Joe," one of the men at the table said to the rosy-cheeked man.

Joe leaned on the bar, cleared his throat, and looked at Jacob.

"Listen, young man, you'd be a fool to travel on to Platkill on a night like this. It's a stretch of empty country with nothing but jagged boulders and thick woods on both sides of the road."

"My horses are good," Jacob said, "and my buggy is in good repair." He stopped and laughed. "And I'm not afraid of driving through a thick woods at night. My friend is expecting me tonight. He'd be worried if I didn't arrive."

There was another stretch of silence as Jacob ate more of his food.

"Go on, Joe, tell him," one of the men urged.

"Now listen to me, young man," Joe began again. "This is strange country around here. It's wild and untamed — not like where I suspect you come from."

"City life can be wild, too," Jacob said with a smile.

"Tell him about Skin-and-Bones, Joe," one of the men said.

"It's not the rocks and the trees I'm trying to warn you about," Joe went on. "It's a creature we call Skin-and-Bones. On nights like this, she likes to trick travelers into giving her a ride. And then they're found the next morning, dead."

Jacob looked from one serious face to another

in the room. Then he burst out laughing.

"You take me for a fool," he said. "I'm not going to be scared by any ghost story."

"But Skin-and-Bones isn't a ghost," Joe said in a deadly serious voice. "She's just skin and bones — almost a skeleton. And when she gets her sharp, bony hands around your neck. . . ."

Jacob threw down his napkin and pushed back his chair. "I've finished my meal, and now I'll be off. Your story was good entertainment. I'll keep it in mind on my journey."

Joe shrugged and took the money Jacob paid him for the meal. Then, as Jacob walked out the door, he called after him, "Good luck. And don't go picking up anybody asking you for a ride."

The cold wind hit Jacob with a blast as he hurried to his buggy. He unhitched the horses and climbed up on the seat. He pulled up the hood as high as it would go to give him shelter from the icy air. Then he slapped the reins against the horses' backs and set off down the road to Platkill.

The last light had faded from the sky, but a full moon lit the road as it snaked through the hills and woods of the rugged landscape. Jacob hummed a song to himself to help keep his spirits up. The cold air was beginning to numb his skin, and his arms were growing tired of holding the horses' reins. And for all his bragging at the inn, he didn't like being out on this deserted road alone at night.

The woods around him were a dense mixture of shadowy fir trees and giant oaks whose bare branches had been stripped of leaves by the wind. Every so often, the buggy would pass an outcropping of rock that gleamed white and ghostly in the moonlight.

Jacob's mind was drifting to thoughts of his friend's warm fireside when, suddenly, his horses let out a strange nickering sound. He looked around him in alarm, and then saw what had upset the horses. A figure was standing by the roadside ahead of him. She had a dark shawl over her head and was reaching out a white arm toward him. The moon was shining on her face, and Jacob could see that it was an old woman beckoning to him.

The story that the men at the inn had told him raced through his mind. His buggy came closer and closer to the woman, but he didn't pull in the reins on his horses. As he passed her by, he saw the look of disappointment on her tired, old face. Jacob thought about turning back to give the woman help, but something inside him whispered that he should go on.

Jacob slapped the reins angrily against the horses' backs and made them race down the road. He felt like a fool. But soon he would reach Platkill and be able to forget all about his journey.

The horses trotted down the lonely road while Jacob shivered on the buggy seat. Then he felt a tension in the reins. The two horses reared back and pranced around on the road, nervous and skittish. It took all Jacob's strength to get them back under control. When they were calm again, he sat on the buggy seat, his heart beating fast, and caught his breath.

Then he saw the slight figure standing by the side of the road. In the moonlight, he could see that she was a young woman with long, reddish-gold hair. She was clutching her green cape around her and looking at him with imploring eyes.

"Sir," she called out. "I need a ride to Platkill. I was thrown off my horse over two hours ago, and I am cold and tired. You're the first person who has come along to help. Could I please have a ride in your carriage?"

Jacob watched the young woman's face as she walked closer. He had seldom seen a woman so lovely, and her voice was soft and refined.

"It would be my pleasure to take you to Platkill," he said, stretching out a hand to help her up onto the buggy seat. "I'm headed there myself tonight, to visit an old friend."

"You're very kind," the young woman said. "I would have frozen in another hour on a night like this."

Jacob pulled his eyes away from her beautiful face that was so close to his now. He slapped the reins on the horses' backs, and the carriage rolled off down the road again.

At first Jacob asked the young woman questions. But she seemed shy and reserved. He realized that she might be frightened of him, a stranger who had picked her up on a lonely road.

For a long while, they traveled on in silence. Every so often, Jacob would glance over at her face. Several times she smiled back at him, her eyes glowing in the moonlight. But then he noticed that her face had set into a hardened expression that didn't change when their eyes met. And even later, when he looked at her,

Jacob thought that she did not look as beautiful as she had at first.

Jacob turned his eyes onto the narrow, dark road in front of him and smiled. Perhaps he had just imagined that she was so beautiful, standing alone on the deserted road in the moonlight. He glanced over at her once more and felt a shock go through his body.

The woman's face no longer looked young. Her skin had lines in it, and her hair looked dull and gray, not reddish gold, in the moonlight. Jacob put the reins in one hand and rubbed his eyes with the other hand. He suddenly felt confused and exhausted. He glanced over to see the woman watching him closely. Her dark eyes seemed to be sunken in their sockets, and her cheekbones stuck out of her thin face.

Jacob shuddered and turned his eyes back to the road. Something was nagging at the back of his mind and making him frightened and nervous. He clenched his teeth and fixed his eyes on the road ahead. According to his calculations, he should be in Platkill in less than fifteen minutes. He would be glad to reach his friend's house and be out of this strange country.

In a flash a prickling feeling started at the back of his neck. It traveled down his spine and then spread through all his body. He willed his eyes to stay on the road, but he could stand it no longer. He turned to look at the woman.

A skeleton sat on the carriage seat beside him, grinning a horrible smile. Jacob knew it was Skin-and-Bones. He gripped the reins in terror and then saw the skeleton's bony hands move out from under her cape and reach for his neck.

Jacob twisted away as Skin-and-Bones's arms lunged for him and clawed at his clothing. He let the reins drop and put his arms up to protect his neck. The bony arms were clutching at him now, and he could barely struggle against their deathly grip. The horses pranced and gallopped wildly down the road.

Jacob felt the sharp, bony fingers closing around his neck. He felt his breath coming in short, desperate gasps. Skin-and-Bones had her face pressed up against his. Jacob pulled together all the life he had left in his body. With a burst of strength he tore away the hands from his neck. Skin-and-Bones reeled back, still grinning her horrible smile. Once again, she lunged for his throat, but Jacob caught her bony wrists in his hands. He wrenched her out of her seat and threw her over the side of the buggy. With a bloodcurdling scream, Skin-and-Bones fell onto the road.

Jacob slumped back in the buggy, half conscious, and let the horses run down the road to Platkill.

"Jacob Cooper, is that you?" a voice was saying.

Jacob opened his eyes to see his friend looking at him with worried eyes.

"Jacob, what's the matter?" his friend asked. "The horses brought you here, but you were unconscious. Are you sick?"

"Skin-and-Bones," Jacob mumbled.

"What nonsense are you talking?" his friend exclaimed.

"Skin-and-Bones," Jacob repeated. "She tried to kill me."

"Did you hear that superstitious old story?" his friend asked, pulling him to the ground. "The local people tell that to frighten travelers."

Jacob rubbed his eyes and looked up at the moonlight. Had it all just been a dream? Then he looked at his friend and saw the expression of horror on his face. Jacob followed his friend's eyes to the side of the buggy.

There, dangling from the hook that had caught it as she fell, was the white, bony hand . . . of Skin-and-Bones.

The Snake Charmer

Lucy Morris sat on the veranda of her parents'
house outside the village of Kampur. Servants
came and went, adding ice to her lemonade or
fetching her a book or treat. Still, Lucy's mouth
was set in a pout. She didn't like this foreign
place. Her father had come here to do research
for three years, but only one month had passed,
and to Lucy, it had seemed like an eternity.

The heavy, humid heat made Lucy feel faint.
The strong, spicy smells of the food made her
lose her appetite. And the insects that scurried
about the house made her scream in terror.

Lucy sat on the veranda pouring out all her
anger into a letter she was writing her friend
back home. Slowly, as she wrote, she became
aware of a sound she hadn't heard before. It

was a tune, a low, whining tune being played on a flute of some kind. Lucy didn't know how long the music had been playing, but once she was aware of it, she could hear nothing else.

She threw down her pen and paper and got up from the big wicker chair where she had been sitting. Then she walked to the end of the veranda that was near the road. The house sat on a dusty, seldom-traveled road that led to the nearby village. Lucy peered down over the veranda railing and caught her breath at what she saw.

On the ground was an old man, dressed in rags, moving back and forth as he played the flute that was making the hypnotic music she heard. The song repeated itself over and over again in high, whining notes. Lucy was about to call to the man to go away when she noticed the basket sitting in front of him. From a hole in its top, a sinister, flat-headed snake was swaying back and forth to the music.

Lucy screamed when she saw the snake. She had a deathly fear of snakes. The man glanced up at her with his dark eyes and then went on playing the song for his cobra.

Lucy ran back into the house and demanded that the servants tell the man to leave at once.

But the servants shook their heads and muttered that it would bring bad luck to them. Lucy wished her mother and father were at home, but they were gone for three days on a research trip. So Lucy ran back out to the end of the veranda and shouted to the old man to go away.

For a moment, he seemed not to hear her. But Lucy kept shouting and motioning to him. Then suddenly he stopped moving and playing the flute and stared at her with his bottomless, black eyes. The cobra suddenly stopped swaying and turned to look at Lucy, too. The snake's evil-looking eyes seemed to be memorizing her face. Lucy shrank back in fear and ran into the house. Once again, the insidious music began.

The music kept up through dinner and into the evening. When Lucy went to bed, she could still hear the song of the snake charmer's flute. In her mind, she could see the cobra swaying back and forth to the music. After hours of tossing and turning in the hot air, she finally fell asleep.

When Lucy woke up, she noticed a change in the air. It was silent. The music had stopped. Lucy ran to her window that looked out onto the road. Looking back up at her from the ground was the snake charmer. When he saw her face he took up his flute and began to play. The music wound its way through the window into Lucy's brain.

At breakfast she threw a temper tantrum and demanded that the servants get rid of the snake charmer. But once again, they refused. They tried to tell her that such a man had strange powers, but she wouldn't listen. She went to the back of the house as far away from the music as she could get.

Lucy stayed inside the house all morning and all afternoon. But still she could not escape the snake charmer's song. Before dinner, she walked out onto the veranda and called to the man.

"I will give you money," she said, "if you'll just go away. What is it you want?"

The man played his song for several more minutes. Then he stopped and looked up at her.

"Something that belongs to you," he said, showing chipped, yellowed teeth. "A lock of your golden hair."

Just then, the cobra reared its head toward Lucy. She shrank back and ran into the house, shutting the door tightly behind her. But the music started up again, like a mad tune in her brain.

Lucy spent another restless night, tossing and turning, and covering her head with a pillow to keep out the sound of the music. She woke so late the next morning that the snake charmer had already started playing by the time she got up. Lucy wasn't sure she could stand it any longer.

She sat down in front of her mirror and started to brush her long, blonde hair. Then she remembered the snake charmer's wish. She picked up a lock of her hair and thought how she would hate to cut it. But if that would get rid of the man and his horrible music, perhaps it would be worth losing.

Lucy searched her drawers for a pair of scissors. She couldn't find one anywhere. She opened her closet doors to see if any were among her childhood toys stored there. At last she found a pair in a box with colored paper and crayons. Then something else caught her eye in the stack of toys in the closet. It was a doll she'd been given when she was six, a doll with long, blonde hair. Her mother had told her the hair was real.

Lucy pulled the doll from her closet and held its head up to hers in front of the mirror. Their hair colors matched perfectly. Lucy laid the doll down on her bed and snipped off a lock of its hair and rushed from the room.

Lucy ran out to the end of the veranda and called to the snake charmer. He kept playing his song until she held up the lock of golden hair for him to see. Then he put down his flute and reached up to take the hair.

Lucy saw the strange look on his face as he took the hair from her hands. She saw the cobra's evil eyes staring at her again. Then the snake showed its short fangs at her.

"Now go away!" she screamed and ran back into the house.

All that morning and afternoon, the house was perfectly still. Just before dinner, a friend of her mother's came to visit Lucy. She said that Lucy's parents would be returning from their trip that night. Lucy felt the happiest she had been since coming to Kampur. She was rid of the snake charmer and his music. And soon her parents would be home.

They came later than she expected, long after dinner was over and when it was almost time for Lucy to go to bed. Lucy hugged her mother and father and then waited for the presents she knew they'd bring. Right after she opened the presents, she began to tell the story of the snake charmer and his endless music.

"But how did you get him to leave?" her mother asked.

"He wanted a lock of my hair," Lucy said. "So I gave him a lock of hair."

"No, Lucy," her father gasped. "You didn't do that! Not to a man like that!"

"Yes, I did," Lucy said. "I gave him a lock of hair. . . ."

She didn't have a chance to finish. Her father jumped to his feet and ran toward her bedroom. Lucy ran after him, trying to tell the rest of her story. But Mr. Morris didn't stop until he reached her bedroom door and threw it open. Lucy ran up beside him as he turned on the lights. Together they stared in horror at the thing on the bed.

Lucy's blonde-haired doll still lay there. And wrapped around it in a death grip . . . was the evil-eyed cobra of the snake charmer.

The Snipe Hunt

The twelve boys sat around the campfire, roasting marshmallows on sticks after finishing their evening meal. Their faces were lit by the jumping flames of the fire — eight older faces and four younger faces. The older boys looked relaxed and confident. But the younger boys looked tense and worried. Tonight they would be tested.

Ty, who was only eleven, was the youngest boy in the group. Jimmy, Paul, and Brad were twelve, but this was their initiation night, too. If they made it through tonight, they'd be let into the camping club.

"What do you think they'll do to us?" Ty whispered to Brad, who sat beside him by the fire.

"I don't know," Brad answered. "Ask Paul. His brother is one of the older guys."

Ty turned to Paul on his other side. "What will they do to us tonight?" he asked in a low voice.

"I heard my brother talk about a snipe hunt," Paul whispered back.

"A snipe hunt?" Ty said. "What's that?"

Before Paul could answer, Mark, one of the leaders, started to talk. Everyone paid attention.

"I want to warn you younger guys about something," Paul began. "These woods are pretty far from civilization. We're out here in the middle of nowhere by ourselves, and we have to be careful. Nobody knows for sure what kind of animals are in the woods — wolves, bears, bobcats. We've had our supper . . . but they might still be hungry."

Ty looked at Brad nervously. Brad's face had grown serious, too.

"And there's another thing I have to tell you," Mark went on. "I heard something on the radio today, just before we left to come here. I've been trying to decide whether or not to tell you, but now I think I should. A murderer escaped from the state penitentiary in Columbus last night. The police haven't caught him yet, but they know he headed in a northwest direction. They figure he's covering about twenty miles a day . . . and, well, you know about where that would take him."

"This place is about twenty miles northwest of Columbus," Brad said.

"Yeah, that's right," Mark said. "But now that we're here, I don't think we should call off our camping trip just because of an escaped murderer."

Ty noticed that his hands were shaking so much that his marshmallow stick was moving up and down. The marshmallow had burned to a crisp.

"So be careful, and report anything strange that you hear or see in the woods," Mark said.

Just then, there was a loud crack in the woods behind the younger boys. They all jumped and turned around.

"What was that?" Ty whimpered.

The older boys laughed.

"What's the matter, Ty, getting a little scared?" Robbie asked.

"It's too early to get scared," Mark said.

"You four guys have to go on your snipe hunt yet. Go to your tents and get a flashlight and get back here in five minutes."

The boys got up from the campfire and walked back to their tents through the chilly night air. The moon was full enough to light their way, but the dark shadows of the trees made it hard to see far into the dense woods. They all got their flashlights from their packs and started back to the campfire.

"Was he telling the truth about the murderer?" Ty whispered to Paul on the way back.

"I don't know," Paul said. "And I don't want to find out."

"I wish this were over with!" Jimmy said.

Mark was waiting for them. He was standing by the fire with four burlap bags.

"These are the bags you use to catch the snipe," he said, handing one to each of the boys.

"How do we know it's a snipe?" Jimmy asked. "What's it look like?"

"Listen, you'll know when you see it," Mark said. "Now be quiet and listen to the rules."

The four boys clutched their bags in one hand and their flashlights in the other and listened.

"Each of you has to walk in a different direction from the campfire," Mark began.

114

"Count how many steps you're taking, and when you get to two hundred fifty, stop. That'll take you far enough away from the light of the campfire. Snipes are too smart to come near a fire."

"What about our flashlights?" Ty asked. "Won't they scare away the snipes?"

Some of the older boys started to laugh. But Mark cut them off.

"Use your flashlights while you're walking out the two hundred fifty steps. Then turn them off and wait."

"How long do we wait?" Brad asked.

"Till we call you in with this whistle," Mark said. He sounded three short whistles and then three long whistles.

"Any questions?"

The four boys looked at each other uneasily.

"What about those other animals you talked about?" Paul said. "What if we see them?"

"Or the murderer?" Ty added with a whisper.

Mark just shrugged his shoulders and looked at his watch.

"Time to start walking," he said. "And remember to count two hundred fifty steps. Then turn off your lights."

Ty glanced over at Paul and Brad and Jimmy. They looked as scared as he felt. Mark told Brad to start walking toward the north. Then he sent Jimmy off to the east and Paul to the west.

"Ty," he said, "you walk south."

Ty gulped, switched on his flashlight, and turned to face the south. He took a step away from the campfire and started counting. At first he took long steps; then he took shorter ones that wouldn't carry him so far into the woods.

Ty had counted a hundred steps when he first turned around. The campfire was just a yellowish glow in the darkness of the woods. He shone his light into the woods in front of him and started walking and counting again. The dead leaves that had fallen from the trees crackled under his feet. Several times a raised root caught at his foot and almost sent him sprawling onto the ground. Night animals scurried away as his light pierced the darkness. Once an owl swooped down across the moon and passed its shadow over him.

Ty had counted two hundred steps. He turned around. The thick trees blocked out the campfire now. He couldn't hear the older boys' voices and laughter anymore. He hoped he would be able to hear Mark's whistles.

Fifty more steps to go. Ty forced his legs to go on through the woods until he had counted to two hundred fifty. Then he swung his flashlight around in the place where he had stopped. It was a small clearing that had a thick carpet of leaves covering the ground.

The flashlight picked up the outline of a big tree stump about three yards from where Ty stood. Tall hickory trees with shaggy bark stood around the small clearing. Ty pointed the light up and saw their long limbs reaching up to the sky like the arms of skeletons. Then he flicked off the flashlight and crouched down on the ground. He clutched the burlap bag in both hands and waited. The snipe hunt had begun.

The wind blew through the tree branches above him, making a strange rattling sound. Ty waited and waited. Once he saw a big shadow move near the tree stump. He froze, not sure if it was a bear or a man. But the shadow disappeared and didn't come back again. Ty's hands were growing numb with cold and fatigue. He thought he would go crazy if he had to stay out in the dark alone one more minute.

Then he heard a strange noise come from the

direction of the tree stump. It was a shrill animal sound, unlike anything he'd ever heard before. He strained his eyes to see in the moonlight. He glimpsed the pale, gray body of an animal walking toward him from the tree stump. It kept making its shrill call as it slowly wobbled across the bed of leaves.

Ty had never seen an animal like it before. He knew it must be a snipe. He leaned over and set the burlap bag down in front of where the animal was walking. It didn't seem to be able to see the bag and headed straight toward it. Ty held his breath until the small animal had walked into his bag. Then he shut the opening of the bag and gripped it tight.

A minute later, three short whistles and three long whistles cut through the stillness of the night. Ty picked up his flashlight and started to run in the direction of the sound. He held the sack away from his body and listened as the animal begin to make shrill noises in a panic.

Ty burst into the light of the campfire with his breath coming in short gasps. Everyone else was standing there, waiting for him. Paul, Brad, and Jimmy had already made it back.

"We thought the murderer might have got you, Ty," Mark said. The boys around the campfire laughed. Ty stood by the fire with his bag, waiting for Mark to ask about the snipe. But Mark didn't even look at his bag.

"The four of you did a great job," he said, looking at Paul, Brad, Jimmy, and Ty. "None of you chickened out. You all passed the test, and now you're in the club."

"But what about the snipe?" Ty asked.

"Come on, Ty, that was just a joke," Robbie said.

"Ty, what do you have in that bag?" Mark asked.

"A snipe," Ty answered.

Just then, the animal cried its weird call.

"He caught something!" Brad said. "Let's see it."

Everyone jumped up and crowded around Ty.

"Drop the bag into this box, Ty," Mark ordered, pulling over an empty food box.

Carefully Ty put the bag into the box and let go of its opening. The other boys peered down into the box. Slowly, the animal Ty had caught crawled out of the bag. It turned its face up at the boys staring down at it. Then it let out a hiss and a shrill screech.

The boys all jumped back.

"What is it?" Robbie asked.

"That's the strangest-looking animal I've ever seen," Mark said.

Again the boys stared down at the animal. It had short gray fur and a thick, stout body. Its paws had sharp white claws and its long tail ended in a jagged point. But its head was weirdest of all. The ears were high and pointed, and the mouth had four long, sharp teeth.

"I think it's a baby that was just born," Mark said. "Its eyes are still shut."

"Look, it's trying to open them," Ty said.

Suddenly the animal's strange eyes flew open. They were orange and glowed in the night.

"Is it a snipe?" Ty asked.

"I don't know," Mark said. "Nobody's ever seen a snipe. We just made up the snipe hunt to scare you guys."

"So what is it?" Brad asked.

The animal started to shriek louder and louder and show its pointed teeth at the boys.

One by one, they backed uneasily away from the box.

"What was that?" Robbie suddenly asked, turning around to look into the woods. "I thought I heard something out there."

"Me, too," said Paul.

The boys fell silent and listened as the animal in the box made its shrill call over and over again. And from different parts of the woods, the same call came back.

"What are we going to do?" Ty asked.

"I don't know," Mark answered, looking scared.

The calls from the woods became louder and louder. Then the leaves on the floor of the woods started to rustle. The boys huddled closer together around the campfire.

Suddenly Ty screamed and pointed to the woods. A pair of strange orange eyes were glowing from the shadows of the trees. They were like the eyes of the animal in the box, only bigger. Then Brad screamed and pointed to the opposite side of the campfire. The boys whirled around and saw another pair of orange eyes glowing in the woods. Then they saw another and another and another.

The animal in the box made a weird noise from deep in its throat. Then from the woods, like a nightmarish echo, came the same noise from all around the boys.

Mark looked at Ty's face, which had turned white with fear.

"You caught a snipe, all right," he said.

Then they turned to look at the orange eyes in the woods. The eyes had started to glow brighter. And they were moving in closer and closer . . . toward the twelve boys huddled together around the campfire.

EVEN MORE TALES FOR THE MIDNIGHT HOUR

For
Genevieve and Gwendolyn

Contents

Voices

It's scary when you think your best friend is
going crazy. That's what I thought about Lara
at first. She would tell me secrets that no one
else knew. Secrets that made chills run up and
down my spine. Then I found out the truth
about the voices. And now I'm worried. . . .

Lara kept the secret to herself for a long
time. I knew something was really wrong with
her. Her face had gotten a drawn, worried look
that never went away. And I could hardly remember when I'd seen her smile last. Then,
one morning in English class, I realized how
sick Lara really was.

She was sitting at the desk right across from
me, staring out the window and looking like
the world had come to an end.

I tore off a piece of paper and wrote her a

quick note. It said: *Why are you acting like somebody died?*

Lara jumped when I nudged her and passed the note. She opened it and seemed to stare at it forever. Then she looked at me with the most frightened expression I'd ever seen on anyone's face.

Just then, Mr. Dudley, our English teacher, asked me to recite the first stanza of Edgar Allan Poe's "The Raven." I stumbled on the first line of the poem but finished the stanza without any trouble. It's one of my favorite poems, but today its eerieness unnerved me.

When Mr. Dudley asked someone on the other side of the room to recite the next stanza, I looked over at Lara again. She had a note ready and slipped it to me when Mr. Dudley wasn't looking.

I unfolded the paper and read the short sentence inside: *There's going to be a bad accident.*

Right away, I looked up from the note to Lara's face. She was staring at me with her big brown eyes full of fear. I looked back down at the note and read the sentence again. Lara had written it like a statement of fact, not a guess or question. I wondered what kind of strange game she was playing with me.

I tore off another piece of my homework paper and wrote: *Are you crazy?* Then I folded it up and threw it onto Lara's desk.

I didn't think Lara could look any worse than she already did, but I was wrong. As soon as she read my note, her face twisted up like she was being pinched with pain. She quickly tore off another scrap of paper and scribbled something on it. Then she passed me the note without meeting my eyes.

As I opened it, I realized my hands were shaking.

You'll see, the note said.

Lara avoided me in school all the rest of the day. I couldn't find her at her locker when classes were over, and I decided to walk home with someone else. That night, I thought about calling her, but something inside held me back.

The next morning, I met Lara's eyes the minute I walked into English class. She was staring straight at the door, as though she were waiting for me. But after I walked into the room, she kept on staring at the same spot. I passed by Mr. Dudley's desk and noticed a substitute teacher standing there. The whole class was buzzing with talk.

As soon as I slipped behind my desk, Meredith turned around in front of me. "Mr. Dudley and his wife were in a terrible car accident last night," she whispered. "His wife might even die. And Mr. Dudley won't be back for a long time."

I felt tears welling up in my eyes. Poor Mr. Dudley. He had been married for only a year, and now he might lose his wife. Suddenly, I felt a shiver pass through my body, and I looked over at Lara. Her dark eyes were shining like hard jewels. And there was a weird little twisted smile on her face.

"See, I'm not crazy," she whispered to me.

I shrank back from her glittering stare. I couldn't believe that this was my best friend whom I'd known since kindergarten. She didn't even seem to feel sorry for Mr. Dudley.

Then the truth hit me like a shock wave. Somehow, Lara had known about the accident before it happened. She had written about it in her note yesterday. I felt so sick that I couldn't look at her all during the rest of the class. I ran from the room before she could get her books together. Then I hung around with a big group of girls for the rest of the day so I wouldn't have to talk to her.

On the way home from school, Lara finally caught up with me. I heard her voice call out my name from down the street, and I wanted to start running. But, instead, I slowed down and tried to stay calm.

"Wait," Lara called again. "I need to talk to you."

I stopped and waited for Lara to catch up. She was panting in a funny way, as though she were out of breath, when she came up to me. Her eyes looked wild, and there was a glossy sheen of perspiration covering her face.

"You're not going out tonight, are you?" she asked in a shaky voice.

"No, of course, not," I said. "I'm studying for my math test tonight. And after that I have to finish my social studies project." I hoped she wasn't going to ask to come over and study with me, because I'd never be able to concentrate with her around.

"Good," Lara said tensely. "Just be sure to stay at home tonight. There's going to be a terrible fire."

I looked at her for a long minute and then blurted out something that I instantly regretted.

"Who's starting the fire — you?"

Lara's face twisted up again like something was torturing her inside.

"They just told me there would be a big fire," she hissed. "I don't know who's starting it."

All of a sudden, I couldn't stand the way she was acting anymore.

I reached over and grabbed her shoulders and shook her.

"What are you talking about, Lara?" I asked, staring straight into her cold, shiny eyes. "Who tells you these horrible things?"

Lara pulled away from me and ran off down the street, never turning around to look back. The rest of the way home, I tried to decide what I was going to do. I could tell my parents about the things she said, or I could talk with the school counselor. But what if they all thought Lara was crazy, too?

That night I stayed at home, even though my little brother begged me to take him to the movies. By 11:00, I had just finished my social studies project. I heard the television news blare out from the living room downstairs. I could hear the sounds of screaming and yelling. I rushed down the steps to see what had happened, my heart pounding with anxiety.

When I saw the television, I knew my worst fears had come true. On the screen, the movie theater downtown was being consumed by the orange flames of a terrible fire. I started to feel sick inside. It had happened again. Somehow, Lara had known about the fire ahead of time.

Finally, I couldn't stand the thoughts that were crowding my brain anymore. I ran to the telephone and dialed Lara's number. After two rings, her mother answered. She told me that Lara couldn't possibly come to the phone. She had been sick in bed all night with a fever, muttering strange things as though she were delirious.

I hung up the phone and stared at the wall. If Lara had been home all night, she couldn't have started the fire. But I knew that she couldn't have just guessed it was going to happen. Not that and the car accident, too.

Lara wasn't in school the next day. All the other kids were talking about the movie theater fire. Luckily, it had happened between shows. But the police hadn't found any clues as to who had started it.

I went through my classes in a daze, torn between wanting to keep Lara's secret and wanting to blurt it out to anyone who would listen. Finally, the last bell of the day rang; and, while I walked home, I decided to tell my parents about Lara. But as soon as I walked through the front door, I saw my mother waiting in the hallway with a worried look on her face.

"Lara's in the hospital," she said softly. "She's very sick. And she's been asking for you."

I felt a chill run through me as I dropped my books on the hallway table and followed my mother out to the car. I wanted to do everything that I could to help Lara, but now I was really afraid.

We drove to the hospital in silence. Mom tried to start conversations, but my mind was occupied with thoughts of Lara. What if she told me another one of her secrets? What would I do about it?

As I walked into Lara's hospital room, my heart started to pound at the sight of her on the bed. Her face had been drained of color, but her eyes were shining like bright little stones with a glint of red in the very middle.

When Lara saw me, she beckoned to me to come closer. I walked up to the side of the bed and leaned over her. But Lara reached up and pulled my head down even closer to hers.

"They say I'm going to die," she whispered in my ear.

"The doctors?" I asked in a trembling voice, afraid to meet her eyes.

"No, the voices," Lara said. "The voices say I'm going to die . . . very soon."

I was shaking now and wanted to run out of the room. But Lara had been my best friend, and I knew she needed me.

"There aren't any voices, Lara," I said, trying to calm her. "And you're going to get better."

I pulled my head away to look at her. The little twisted smile gave her pale face a scary expression.

"I'm not crazy," she whispered. "They talk to me all the time, the voices do."

Suddenly, she grabbed the back of my neck and pulled my head down next to hers. Then she hissed in my ear.

"Listen!"

I screamed and pulled my head away. Then I stared down at Lara as she slumped against the pillow with her eyes shut and a smile of contentment on her face.

The voices told me that I should stay and say good-bye to Lara, because it would be the last time I would ever see her. But I thought if I started running, I could get away from them.

I was wrong. The voices have been talking to me for two months now. And I'm worried. Everything they've told me has come true. And lately, they've been talking about an accident. They're trying to make me guess who the victim will be. But I think I already know.

The Gecko

Jason flicked on the light switch in his kitchen and, with a shudder, watched the cockroaches scurry into hiding. One slipped under the toaster. Another ran into a food cabinet. Two more disappeared behind the refrigerator.

The sight of the cockroaches made Jason's stomach turn. He had wanted to make an evening snack, but now the thought of food repulsed him. What if a cockroach was in the bread drawer? What if one scurried out from the refrigerator when he opened the door?

Jason flicked off the light again and crept back into his living room. He stared at the white walls of the small room, thinking how it looked like a prison cell with its windows barred against robbers. Jason shook his head and asked himself why he had ever come to

New York City. It was a cold, lonely place to be if you didn't have friends or a family. Jason thought he could almost stand the loneliness if it weren't for one thing — the cockroaches. His apartment was infested by hundreds and hundreds of them.

The roaches made him feel like a prisoner in his own home. At first, he had tried to kill them with a shoe or a newspaper. But they were always too fast, and they could always find somewhere to hide. Now, whenever he saw one, he ran away from it — from the kitchen into the living room, from the living room into the bedroom. But the roaches never let him alone. Only when he was asleep at night could Jason rid his brain of their quick, scurrying bodies.

Jason eased himself down onto his couch and carefully picked up the newspaper. Very slowly, he opened it and shook out the pages. Once, a roach had jumped out from the sports section but, tonight, the paper was safe. Jason glanced over the front section, reading the headlines and editorials. Then he turned to the second section and, immediately, a headline caught his eye. He leaned forward in anticipation as he read through the article. Then, with a nervous smile playing on his lips, he pulled out a notebook from his jacket pocket and wrote down an important word he had just learned. GECKO.

Jason couldn't stop thinking about the article all through work the next day. Finally, at 5:00, he left the office and hurried to the pet store that he always passed on his way home. He ran the last block just to be sure he got there before it closed. After pushing open the front door, Jason walked past the fish and hamsters and kittens in the front of the store. He went down the crowded corridor to the back, where the more exotic, and less popular, pets were kept.

There, beside a case full of snakes, Jason found the gecko. It sat alone in its glass case, staring at him with its green, popped-out eyes. Jason stared at its brown-striped body covered with scaly bumps. It was bigger, much bigger, than he thought it would be. Then, suddenly, the lizard jumped up toward Jason onto the side of the glass and stuck there. With a mixture of disgust and fascination, Jason studied the sticky pads on each of the gecko's feet. He had read about those in the article. With them, the gecko could climb up any smooth surface, even a ceiling.

The gecko's cold stare and scaly body turned Jason's stomach. But then he saw the sign hanging on the bottom of its case; it read: COCK-

ROACH KILLER. That was why Jason had come to the pet store to find this strange animal. In the newspaper he had read that one gecko could eat ten, twenty, even thirty cockroaches a night. It got its name, the article said, from the high-pitched bark it made, especially after eating its prey. Jason took a final look at the lizard and decided he had to buy it, no matter how big and ugly it was.

A sales assistant walked by just then and asked to help him. Jason asked her if this was a normal-sized gecko. She admitted that it had grown quickly and was bigger than usual. But she pointed out that its size would make it an even hungrier hunter. Hesitantly, Jason said he would buy it. A short time later, he walked out of the store with the gecko in a clear plastic carrying case.

When Jason walked into his apartment that night, he flicked on the lights and quickly looked around for the scurrying bodies that greeted him each time he came home. Ten, he counted. Ten cockroaches by the front door alone. They crept into cracks in the floor and hid under the living room furniture. Jason gritted his teeth and walked into the apartment. He set the gecko down on the small, round table that he used for eating and working. Immediately, the lizard jumped onto the side of the plastic case, staring up at him with its weird green eyes.

Jason shrugged off his coat and sat down on a chair in front of the gecko. He pulled out the newspaper article from his jacket pocket. "The Perfect Pet for the City Dweller — the Hungry Gecko," the headline read. Jason skimmed through the article again to read what he was supposed to do with the gecko next. According to the writer, all he had to do was let the gecko loose in his apartment. Unlike most pets, it required no care. It fed itself on cockroaches. And, in fact, an owner seldom saw the gecko again. It only came out at night — in the dark — to hunt its prey.

Jason noticed that his hands were trembling as he laid the article down on the table. He hesitated and then reached up to lift off the top of the plastic case. Just as he touched the lid, the gecko leapt up and stuck onto it. Jason jerked his hands away and stared at the ugly lizard. Suddenly, the thought of it loose in his apartment made his skin crawl. Then, out of the corner of his eye, he saw yet another cockroach scurry across the floor. That settled it.

Jason quickly reached over to the plastic case and flipped open the lid. The gecko froze for a moment under the bright light. Its scaly tail flicked back and forth. Its green eyes darted around the room. Then it suddenly sprang up and leapt onto the floor near the cockroach. Within seconds, the gecko had chased the cockroach under the refrigerator and disappeared from sight.

Jason sat silently for a moment, stunned by the thought of what he had done. Now a lizard was hiding in the dark places of his apartment along with the cockroaches. He tried to comfort himself by picking up the newspaper article and reading it again. Finally, with wary steps, he walked into the kitchen and began to make himself dinner.

Jason took his food into the living room and sat down in front of the television to eat. He watched a long movie that took his mind off the gecko until he flicked off the set at midnight. Feeling strangely exhausted, he stumbled into his bedroom and got ready for the night.

Jason lay down in bed and shut his eyes, feeling as though he could sleep forever. As sleep began to slowly steal over his mind, a strange crunching sound suddenly broke the silence of the apartment. Crunch, crunch, crunch. Jason's body tensed, and then he sat bolt upright in bed. He strained his ears, waiting for the sound to come again. Crunch, crunch, crunch. A second later, a weird bark pierced the quiet of the night, shattering Jason's nerves. GECKO. GECKO. GECKO.

The sound of the gecko's bark made Jason's blood run cold. He fell back in bed and pulled the covers up tightly around his neck. His mind fled back to the newspaper article. It had never mentioned the horrible crunching sound that the gecko made as it ate the hard shells of the cockroaches. And it had never said how loud the gecko barked. Then Jason remembered that his gecko was bigger than most. Maybe that was why it was so loud.

Crunch, crunch, crunch. The gecko was eating another cockroach. The sound scratched at Jason's brain like fingernails against a chalkboard. He buried his head under a pillow, but even the pillow couldn't keep out the gecko's bark of triumph as it swallowed its prey.

The next morning, Jason stumbled into the bathroom and stared at his drawn, white face in the mirror. A strange glint played in his dark eyes, and his lips were pale and pulled down at the corners into an anxious grimace. He wondered if anyone would notice how he looked at work today. He wondered how he would get through the day at all.

When he finally left the office at 5:00, Jason began to follow his old route home. But, as he drew closer and closer to his building, the slower and slower he walked. He didn't want to go back to his apartment, where the gecko was waiting for him in the dark.

Jason stopped at a small Italian restaurant to eat an inexpensive meal of spaghetti for dinner. Afterward, he went to see a double-feature at a movie theater, which lasted for four hours. Finally, just before midnight, he pushed open the door to his apartment. As Jason flicked on the entrance light, a weird bark shattered the silence. He jumped and then looked straight up at the ceiling just above his head. The gecko's striped body was pressed there; it was crunching on a half-dead cockroach.

For a few seconds, Jason stared at it in horror. The gecko seemed to have grown during the day, and it was staring at him as though it was still hungry. Jason ran for his bedroom and slammed the door shut. He locked it behind him and stood shaking in the dark. The gecko couldn't have followed him in that quickly, he told himself. He was safe here in the bedroom.

Nervously, he undressed, slipped into bed, and lay there trembling. He tried to calm his nerves and soothe his mind into sleep. There would be no crunching tonight, he told himself. No crunching. No barking. Only sleep.

Then, out of the darkness, came the sound. Crunch, crunch, crunch. Jason screamed in panic as his nerves snapped. The gecko was somewhere in the room, hunting and eating. He buried his head under the covers; but, still, he couldn't shut out the gecko's bark as it set off to find another victim in the dark bedroom.

The next morning, Jason watched his shaking hands spill coffee from his cup. Again, the gecko had kept him awake almost all the night with its murderous crunching and barking. But Jason noticed that there was only one cockroach in the kitchen that morning. And there had been none in the bathroom. Slowly but surely, the gecko was stalking and killing them, one by one, through the long nights.

Just then, Jason saw the gecko dart from his bedroom into the kitchen. He choked back a scream as he saw the gecko's bloated body barely squeeze under the refrigerator. It had grown even bigger during the night. Suddenly, Jason put down his coffee and stared at the wall as a new thought crept into his mind. What would happen if the gecko ran out of roaches to eat?

By the end of the week, Jason could not find one roach anywhere in the apartment, no matter how hard he searched. There were none in the refrigerator. None scurried away when he came in the door at night. None hid under the wastebasket in the bathroom or inside the magazines on his nightstand. Jason had noticed something else. The gecko's crunching had become louder and louder but less and less frequent during the night. Still, Jason had not slept. Now the silence worried him as much as the crunching had.

That evening, Jason watched television until his eyes burned with fatigue. Finally, he crept into his bedroom and lay there perfectly still in the dark. He waited and waited for the crunching sound to come. But the room was quiet, as quiet as a tomb. In his mind, Jason pictured all the places where the gecko might be. Was it lurking on the dusty floor under his refrigerator? Was it pressed up against the warm glass of his television screen? Or was it in his dark bedroom? Maybe it was crawling across the ceiling above him at this very moment. Maybe it was hungry.

Late that night, the police rushed into the apartment building to answer a call from Jason's next-door neighbor. She reported terrible screams coming from his apartment, followed by a weird crunching sound and then a blood-curdling bark.

The police broke down Jason's locked door

and searched the apartment. Jason was nowhere to be found. His bed was empty except for a few suspicious stains on the sheets. And although they looked everywhere else, the police forgot to look under the bed. There, hiding in the dark, was the bloated gecko, full at last.

The Head

Jenny knew there was something wrong with the house the minute she saw it. It looked neglected, with its shutters hanging crooked and its paint peeling around the old-fashioned windows. Inside, too many things were half done, as though someone had started them and then left quickly before they were finished. Most of all, Jenny didn't like the way the thick woods came right up around the sides of the house. The trees made the rooms seem dark and shadowy, as though they were hiding secrets.

It was the week before school started when Jenny and her parents drove down the long lane to the old house, pulling a trailer full of their belongings behind them. Her parents had left the city because they wanted Jenny to grow up in a place where she could be safe and breathe fresh air. They were disappointed about the looks of the house, too, but insisted that Jenny should be happy there. After all, they had moved for her own good.

On their first evening in the house, Jenny was surprised by how quickly darkness came. It seemed as though there was no twilight at all. The thick woods blocked out the sunset and the trees cast long shadows against the house.

Jenny helped her parents set the table for a celebration dinner in the old dining room. But when they sat down to eat, Jenny couldn't shake off her feeling of gloom.

"Cheer up," her father said. "You'll get used to it here. Tomorrow you can run around outside and breathe in the fresh air."

Jenny stared at him over the flames of the candles in the middle of the table. He didn't seem to understand how bad the house was. Either that, or he was just refusing to admit it.

"Eat your dinner, Jenny," her mother said softly. "You'll feel better after a good night's sleep."

Silently, Jenny ate her food and stared out the big dining room windows that looked into the woods. The glow of the candles flickered against the panes like little golden eyes.

Jenny watched the shadows of the trees shift in the deep blue sky. Then, suddenly, she saw a strange shape move from one tree to another. She stopped eating and watched it. The shape moved again, and again. At first, Jenny thought it might be some kind of large animal. Then the shape moved closer and closer to the house. Jenny gasped as it began to walk up to the window. Now she could see that it was a human figure, a woman's figure. But it had no head.

Jenny dropped her fork and started to scream. She pointed to the window, but before her parents could rush over to look, the figure faded into the shadows of the night.

Jenny sat at the table, shaking. "I saw it, I really did," she cried. "It was a woman without a head."

Her father came away from the window and put his arm around her. Jenny saw him exchange a worried look with her mother. She could tell that they didn't believe her.

Later that night, Jenny walked up the narrow staircase to her new bedroom, clasping one of her favorite books in her hands. She turned on a lamp and looked around the strange room. The old wallpaper was a faded yellow, and the windows were still bare and curtainless. Her mother had promised to buy shades as soon as they were settled in.

Jenny crawled between the covers and began

to read her book to keep away the horrible thoughts that tried to crowd her mind. An hour later, her mother came into the room, kissed her good-night, and turned off the reading light.

"It's time to go to sleep, Jenny," she said. "And don't worry. It's always difficult to move, but you'll get over it in time."

"Leave the door open a little," Jenny asked as her mother left the room, "just in case . . ."

Jenny shut her eyes and tried to drift off to sleep. But a summer storm had sprung up, and the wind was moaning through the trees and howling around the house. Tree branches flailed in the air and scratched against the roof. Then a tapping began against the far window of Jenny's room. She told herself that it was just a branch hanging near the house. But in her imagination, it became something much worse.

The tapping went on and on. Finally, Jenny couldn't stand it any longer. She crawled out of bed and slowly tiptoed to the window. Looking out into the moonlit sky, she saw a branch from a nearby tree hit against the window and make the tapping sound. Jenny breathed a sigh of relief and then glanced down at the ground below the tree. She saw something that made her blood run cold.

Standing beneath her window in the stormy night was the headless woman. Her hands were held high as though she were reaching up to Jenny. And her neck was nothing but a bloody stump.

Jenny let out a piercing scream and ran back to her bed, sick with fear. She kept screaming until her parents ran into the room and flicked on the light.

"It was her again," Jenny cried, "the headless woman. She was right out there, below my window."

Her parents ran over to the window and searched the darkness. But all they could see were the trees swaying in the wind.

"Jenny, you have to get hold of yourself," her father said sternly as he came over to her bed. "You aren't going to make us move back to the city by making up these ridiculous stories." He flicked off her light again and led her mother out of the room.

Jenny pulled the covers up over her head and cried in the darkness. The haunting figure of the headless woman was still in her mind as she fell asleep; then it drifted through her nightmares like an evil omen.

The next day, her parents tried to keep Jenny busy with unpacking boxes of books and clothes and dishes. As the bright sun shone through the front windows of the house, Jenny slowly began to relax and wonder if it hadn't all been her imagination. By late afternoon, she actually found herself smiling and looking forward to going out to dinner that night.

The family drove into a nearby small town to see the middle school where Jenny would go in less than a week. Then they found a charming little restaurant that served homemade food. While eating their meal, Jenny's parents struck up a conversation with a middle-aged woman who had come into the restaurant shortly after they'd arrived. She introduced herself as Mrs. O'Leary and welcomed them to town. She explained that she was a widow who did housecleaning and baby-sitting to help make ends meet. Jenny wished her parents would stop talking to the woman. Mrs. O'Leary had curly red hair that looked dyed, and she treated Jenny as though she were a little child.

To Jenny's dismay, her mother suddenly asked Mrs. O'Leary if she could come out to their house the next evening to stay with Jenny. There was a parents' meeting at the middle school, she explained, and she didn't want to leave Jenny alone in the new house. Mrs. O'Leary eagerly accepted.

As they walked out to the car, Jenny turned to her mother angrily. "I don't need a baby-sitter, Mom," she said. "I wish you would have asked me about it first."

"I know you don't need a sitter," her mother said. "But it won't hurt to have a little company around, just in case . . ."

Her mother didn't finish what she had started to say. They drove the rest of the way home in an awkward silence.

After unpacking several more boxes later that night, Jenny started to go up to bed. But, as she climbed the steps, she suddenly remembered that she had left her book in the car. She asked her father to go out and get it, but he insisted that she get it herself.

Jenny opened the front door and peered out at the shed, where the car was parked about twenty yards from the house. She could see the roof of the shed silhouetted against the night sky, where a half-moon rode among the shadowy clouds.

Jenny dashed from the front steps of the house down the path to the shed, passing by the tall trees that grew on both sides. It took only a few moments to reach the car. She opened the back door and found the book on the seat just where she had left it. Clutching it tightly in her hands, Jenny started back.

She slowed down to look at the house in the dark for the first time. There were so many windows, she noticed, so many windows that someone could come through if they weren't carefully locked. Jenny shuddered and started to run.

Just then, a dark shadow moved out of the trees in front of her. Before she could stop, Jenny ran right into it. She felt herself hit a woman's warm body. Its arms reached out and wrapped around her. Jenny looked up and saw the bloody stump of the headless woman's neck, only inches from her face.

She screamed and twisted out of the woman's grasp. The arms grabbed at her again in the darkness, but Jenny got away from them and stumbled toward the house. Sobbing hysterically, she ran inside and screamed for her parents.

"It was her again, the headless woman," Jenny cried. "She tried to grab me."

Her parents held Jenny and reassured her that everything would be all right. Her father promised to take her as soon as possible to a doctor who would understand her problem.

All the next day, Jenny stayed in bed. Her parents let her get up for dinner and sit quietly on the couch until Mrs. O'Leary arrived. When the woman came, Jenny's parents took her into the kitchen for a private conversation. Jenny could just imagine what they were saying. But she felt better about Mrs. O'Leary being in the house. She didn't want to be left alone there tonight.

After her parents drove away, Jenny stayed downstairs on the couch while Mrs. O'Leary curiously wandered from one room to another in the house.

"Have you ever been here before?" Jenny asked the woman when she came into the living room.

"As a matter of fact, I used to live here," Mrs. O'Leary answered bluntly, "before my husband died."

For a minute, Jenny was shocked that Mrs. O'Leary hadn't mentioned this before to her parents. But the woman didn't seem to think it was important.

"Who lived here after you moved?" Jenny asked.

"Any number of renters, like yourself," the woman said. "But it never seems to work out for them. After several weeks, they all leave."

Jenny felt a chill creep over her as she wondered why the other renters left. Had the headless woman always haunted the house?

"You don't look well," Mrs. O'Leary said, staring at Jenny's face. "Perhaps you should go back up to bed. Your parents told me that might be necessary."

"Maybe you're right," Jenny said, getting up from the couch. She was surprised to feel her legs shaking under her.

"You go on up, and I'll bring you a cup of hot chocolate later," Mrs. O'Leary said.

Jenny nodded her head and began to climb the staircase to her room. She lay down in bed, feeling strangely exhausted. Then she picked up the new novel she had started and began to read. The time passed without her even knowing it, until, suddenly, she remembered that Mrs. O'Leary had promised to bring her up some hot chocolate. Once she thought of it, she couldn't get it out of her mind.

Jenny crawled out of bed and walked over to a chair by the window where she had thrown her warmest sweater. The night had grown chilly, and she was beginning to shiver. As she bent down to pick up the sweater, Jenny glanced out the window at the ground below. There, pacing back and forth beneath her window, was the headless woman.

For a second, Jenny's mind froze in terror. Then she ran away from the window and began to scream Mrs. O'Leary's name. She called and called until she was hoarse, but the woman never came. Finally, Jenny couldn't stand being in the room alone anymore. Frantically, she ran down the stairs and into the living room, where she had been sitting with Mrs. O'Leary.

The couch and the chairs were empty. But on the coffee table in the middle of the room was Mrs. O'Leary's head. Its curly red hair rested on the wooden table. Its dark eyes stared at Jenny and followed her into the room. Then its thin lips widened into a mocking smile.

Jenny screamed and started to run back upstairs. But, just then, Mrs. O'Leary's headless body walked back into the house, her arms stretched out to catch Jenny.

Better Late Than Never

One morning, John O'Rourke found himself walking along a busy downtown street. He stared around at the shops and cars in confusion, having no idea why he was there or where he was going. It seemed as though he had suddenly wakened from a dream and found himself back in reality.

Coming around a corner, John looked straight ahead at the brilliant morning sun hovering low in the sky. The light almost blinded him and sent a sharp pain through his head. He pressed his hand against his forehead and then drew it away, noticing the dark red flakes on it. Strange, he thought, the flakes looked almost like dried blood.

Feeling suddenly weak, John sat down on the curb and tried to understand what was happening to him. A few seconds later, a car sped by, almost hitting him. John jerked back and tried to jump to his feet. But his body was so sore that he had trouble just standing up. He brushed off the dust from his clothes and noticed that he was wearing his best suit and a pair of highly polished shoes. But when he pulled up his coat sleeve to check the time, he found that he wasn't wearing his watch. That was the strangest thing of all. John O'Rourke never took his watch off, not even to sleep. Being on time was an obsession with him.

Now, more than ever, he felt lost and confused. What was he doing here in the middle of town? And what time was it? John began to wander aimlessly down the street. Ahead of him on the sidewalk he recognized the woman who worked in his dentist's office. He walked up behind her and tapped her shoulder.

"Excuse me, Mrs. Anderson, could you tell me the time? I don't seem to have my watch on."

The woman whirled around at the sound of his voice. Her eyes widened as she stared at his face. Then, with a piercing scream, she ran away down the street.

John stood frozen in place on the sidewalk, watching her flee. He asked himself why her face had contorted with fear at the sight of him. Was there something horrifying about the way he looked? Passing his hand over his face, he felt a strange bump on his forehead. And, once again, he saw the dark red flakes on his hand.

John turned and walked toward the large glass window of a store along the sidewalk. His reflection wavered in it, looking ghostly in the morning light. There seemed to be a strange, dark bruise on his forehead, and his face looked as white as the stiffly starched shirt he wore.

John walked on in the direction of the street where he lived with his wife in a small, two-bedroom house. They had never had children because John had forbidden it. He was sure that children would upset his schedule and make him late. Being late was something he could not tolerate.

Now, for some reason that he didn't understand, John felt sure that he was going to be late for an extremely important appointment. He knew his wife could tell him what it was, and she would have a warm breakfast waiting. It was odd, though, he didn't feel in the least bit hungry.

Just then, a school bus rumbled by, and John stared up into its windows. Staring back at him was Lucy Potter, the little girl who lived next door. John saw her raise her hand and point at him. Her mouth was open wide as though she were laughing, or screaming. A moment later, every child's face in the windows was staring at him. John glared at the bus as it moved down the street. Obviously, he had been right not to have children if they all acted that rudely.

John found that his knees were growing weaker and weaker. He began to wish that someone he knew would drive by so that he could wave them down and ask them for a ride. John slumped against the pole of a stoplight near a street corner and stared up the road. In the distance he saw a bright yellow car that he recognized. It belonged to his secretary, Miss Spencer. John stood up straight and waved his arms. Luckily, the stoplight turned red just as the car approached.

The bright yellow car slowed down to a stop at the light, but Miss Spencer was busy looking in the rearview mirror as she put on her lipstick. John walked out into the street and tried to open the door on the passenger's side. It was locked. He rapped his knuckles on the window and peered in at Miss Spencer. She stared back at him with a look of horror on her face; then she gripped the steering wheel and pressed down on the gas pedal. The car shot forward through the red light, throwing John onto the street.

Vowing to fire Miss Spencer the first chance he got, John picked himself up and limped back to the sidewalk. His head was throbbing with pain now. He looked down at his trembling hands and saw that the skin was pale, pale as ivory, and so dry that it was almost brittle.

John staggered over to a storefront with a mirrored window and looked into it. There were dark circles around his sunken eyes. His lips seemed drained of color and wouldn't move when he tried to smile. His skin seemed to reflect the bluish color of the bruise on his forehead.

A dark fear spread through John's body, followed by the strange sense of panic. He was going to be late. And whatever appointment he had, he couldn't miss it.

Behind him, John saw a telephone booth reflected in the mirror. That was the answer. He could call his wife and have her come get him. She could check his calendar and find out where it was that he had to be.

John walked as quickly as his stiff legs would carry him to the telephone booth. He slipped inside and shut the door behind him. For a moment, he was overcome by a wave of claustrophobia. The booth was so narrow; it felt almost like a coffin.

John fumbled in his pockets for a coin, but they were empty. Then he saw a shiny quarter left behind by the last person using the phone. He slipped it into the money slot and pushed the buttons for his home phone number.

The first ring of the phone sounded very, very far away. John found himself struggling to breathe. The air seemed dead in the small telephone booth. The phone in his house rang a second time. His wife usually answered right after the second ring. But, still, there was only silence, a stifling, lonely silence.

John didn't think he could stay in the narrow booth another second. His hands began to claw desperately at the handle of the door. Finally, he heard a clicking sound on the other end of the telephone line. The receiver was being picked up. A strange woman's voice said, "Hello."

"Is . . . is Mrs. O'Rourke there?" John gasped.

The woman didn't answer for a moment. Then, in an anxious voice, she said, "Oh no, Mrs. O'Rourke just left for the funeral. Haven't you heard? Her husband died two days ago in a car accident downtown."

John didn't hear any more of what the woman said. The phone slipped out of his white bony hands and dangled from its cord. Then John pushed open the door of the telephone booth and lunged out.

He would have to hurry. But he could still get to the graveyard on time.

The Golden Arm

Once there was a woman who had a golden arm. She had lost her real arm in a terrible accident. But after she got the golden arm, she didn't even seem to miss her real one.

The golden arm was beautifully made. It was slender and elegant and shone with a warm glow from its shoulder down to its fingertips. The woman vainly decorated its gold fingers with jeweled rings. People who saw her thought she must be very rich to have such a lovely golden arm. But, in fact, the opposite was true.

The woman's husband made only enough money for them to get by modestly in life. For many years, he had carefully saved part of his paycheck. This money had added up to a considerable sum. But after her accident, his wife had demanded that he spend it all on the golden arm and its decorations. Being a meek person, he did as she asked. But, deep inside, he hated the arm.

Every morning, at the breakfast table, the man would stare at the golden arm lying on the table across from him. He would think of all the scrimping and saving he had done over the years. He would think of all the comforts the money could have brought him. Now it all rested in his wife's golden arm. He grew to hate its shapely curves and shiny gold fingers.

As the years passed, the woman seemed to grow more and more fond of her golden arm and less and less fond of her husband. She insisted on a new ring every birthday. Her husband, afraid of her terrible temper and biting tongue, scrimped and saved again to meet her wishes. But, with each passing year, his resentment against the arm grew and grew.

One cold winter evening, as the couple was reading the newspaper, the wife read a notice about the death of a woman she had gone to school with. She dropped the paper suddenly and stared blankly at the wall, her face drained of color. The idea of death had crept into her mind, and it would not go away. The more the woman thought about dying, the more she found herself stroking the golden arm with her other hand. Slowly, an idea began to take form in her mind, an idea she had not considered before. She turned to her husband and met his eyes with a steely gaze.

"If I happen to die before you," she said to him, "promise to bury me with my golden arm."

Her husband clutched his newspaper so tightly that it ripped, and he stared at his wife in shocked amazement.

"But that arm is the only thing of value that we have," he said, his voice shaking. "All the money I've worked for and saved has gone into it."

"I want to be buried with it," his wife said in an insistent voice. "And I want all my rings on the fingers." She paused, picturing in her mind how she would look in her casket. "Just think how people will stare when they view my body."

At that very moment, the husband's heart turned as hard and cold as the golden arm. Any feelings of love that remained for his wife were turned to bitter disgust. But, still, he was afraid to cross her. Calmly, he looked her in the eye and promised to do as she asked. After all, he told himself, there was little chance that she would die before he did, anyway.

The future, however, proved him wrong. Just one year later, his wife died suddenly of a mysterious disease. In shock, the man went about the preparations for her funeral. He planned to tell the undertaker to remove the golden arm before laying his wife out in the casket. But then his wife's relatives arrived to help make the funeral arrangements. To his dismay, she had told them about her desire to be buried with the golden arm. She had even given them a signed, legal document stating her wishes. And, so, even in death, his wife got her way.

At the funeral, the man stared at the body laid out in the coffin, with the golden arm gleaming at its side. On the golden fingers sparkled all her jeweled rings. And as the coffin lid was closed for the final time, the man said goodbye, not to his wife, but to his life savings.

After the funeral, the man's mind settled into a heavy gloom that wouldn't lift. Day after day, he thought of his wife's coffin and the golden arm gleaming inside it. Why, he asked himself, should she still have the arm when he could sell the gold and live out the rest of his life without worry. Slowly, the man's meekness and timidity turned to anger and revenge.

Then, on one cold and windy night while he lay in bed, an idea began to prey on the man's mind. What if the arm was no longer in the coffin? What if someone had already stolen it?

After all, who would be so foolish as to let that much gold stay buried? The idea took root in the man's mind and grew there like a poisonous weed.

Finally, not able to stand it any longer, the man jumped from his bed and pulled on his warmest clothes. He went out to the garage and found a pick and shovel. Then he hurried toward the graveyard in which his wife was buried under the hard, cold ground.

Breathing heavily with anticipation and fear, the man came up to the high iron gates of the graveyard. He hesitated and then pushed against them. The gates swung open like the jaws of a gigantic black mouth. Only the thought of the golden arm made the man force his legs forward, step by step, toward his wife's grave. His mind was still obsessed by the picture of the grave, dug up and disturbed. But when he reached the burial site, the grave lay tranquilly under the full moon, covered by bouquets of wilting flowers.

In a mad frenzy, the man began to work. He dug the pickax into the hard earth and then shoveled it away, digging deeper and deeper. At last, the pick struck the top of his wife's expensive coffin. An image of the golden arm began to burn in the man's mind. It gave him enough courage to pull open the coffin lid and look down at his wife's decaying body. In triumph, he pulled the golden arm from the grave and cradled it against his chest.

Quickly, the man shut the coffin back up and covered it again with the cold earth. Then, with a frightened gleam in his eyes, he hurried away from the graveyard, clutching the golden arm under his coat.

The night had turned bitter cold. Rain began to lash down on the man's head as he ran back to his house. He hugged the golden arm tighter and tighter under his coat, but its icy embrace sent a shudder through his whole body.

At last, the man reached his home, feeling sick with fear. He searched and searched for a place to hide the arm, but nowhere seemed safe. Finally, in desperation, he slipped it under the blankets of his bed and crawled in beside it.

Outside, the wind howled around the house, and the rain tapped like angry fingers against the windowpanes. The man huddled in his bed and tried to calm his shaking body. He pulled the covers up higher around his face, but, beside him, the golden arm was still icy cold. It seemed to draw all the heat out of his body, making him feel like a corpse in a coffin.

When sleep refused to come, the man tried to busy his mind by thinking of all the things he would buy after selling the golden arm. But, his mind was pulled away from these thoughts by a soft, strange wail that seemed to come and go with the howling of the wind. The man sat up in bed and strained his ears. Then he heard the sound again, just outside the window.

WHOOO . . . WHOOO'S GOT MY GOLDEN ARM?

The wailing voice made the man's blood run cold. It sounded like his wife's voice, mixed with the howling of the wind. He looked over to where the golden arm lay beside him in bed, and he shrank away from it.

Again, the man thought he heard the strange voice calling from outside the window. He strained his ears to hear and listened carefully. But the sound faded away into the night with the howling of the wind. Slowly, the man relaxed and smiled at his own stupidity. He told himself that he had let his imagination go wild. But, just then, the wailing started up again, like a ghostly call from the grave.

WHOOO . . . WHOOO'S GOT MY GOLDEN ARM?

In panic, the man searched the darkness. The voice sounded closer now. It seemed to be coming from inside the house. All the man could think about now was hiding the golden arm. He couldn't be discovered with it beside him in bed! Reaching under the covers, the man tried to pick up the arm. But it was so cold that it almost froze his fingers. He dropped it and stared at it in terror. In the pale moonlight, he saw one gold finger pointing at him in accusation. Then, again, the wailing voice echoed into the room.

WHOOO . . . WHOOO'S GOT MY GOLDEN ARM?

Now the voice was coming from the staircase. Then the man heard the sound of footsteps climbing the stairs, one by one, as the wailing voice came closer and closer to his bedroom door.

WHOOO . . . WHOOO'S GOT MY GOLDEN ARM?

With a sickening creak, the door to the bedroom opened. The man lay trembling under the covers, trying to hide from the thing that was coming nearer and nearer to his bed. His teeth began to chatter with fear, and he suddenly felt the icy-cold finger of the golden arm stab at him.

Now the footsteps had reached the bed. The arm's cold grip was reaching up around the man's neck. Then, softly, the voice beside his bed whispered into his ear.

WHO'S GOT MY GOLDEN ARM?

With a scream, the man jumped from the bed and shouted, "I do!"

He was buried beside his wife the next day.

Dead Man's Cave

Jake Lucas stopped on the narrow, shadowy trail that led to Dead Man's Cave. He turned around to face his younger cousin Peter, who was following close behind. Peter's eyes looked scared, and his brown freckles stood out against his pale, sweating skin.

"Where are we going?" Peter asked, his eyes nervously darting from one side of the path to the other.

"You know," Jake answered, staring at him long and hard.

"Come on, Jake, you're just kidding, aren't you?" Peter asked. He looked as though he might start crying at any moment.

"No, I'm not kidding," Jake said. "We're going to Dead Man's Cave." He reached up, snapped off a branch from an overhanging tree, and switched it back and forth in the air.

"But, Jake," Peter pleaded. "You know those stories about Dead Man's Cave. . . ."

"I don't believe those old stories anymore," Jake snapped. "There aren't any ghosts in that old cave. Nothing's going to come out and grab us. Parents just say those things to scare kids."

"Well, if the stories aren't true, then why's it called Dead Man's Cave?" Peter asked.

"Because a bunch of miners were killed there in a cave-in years ago," Jake said, starting down the trail again. "Come on, let's get moving."

He glanced back to see if Peter was following. Peter was right behind him, same as always. Ever since they were little kids, Peter had been like Jake's pet dog, following him everywhere.

Jake hadn't planned on going to Dead Man's Cave today. He had just woken up that morning knowing he was going to do it. Summer vacation was almost over, and when he went back to school, he wanted to have something to brag about to his friends. Most of all, he wanted to do the thing that his father had forbidden most.

Jake stopped again to get his bearings. The trail had led into a stand of fir trees that blotted out the sun overhead. A wind came out of nowhere, stirring the branches up and down like huge flapping arms.

"How do you know where we're going?" Peter asked in a trembling voice.

"This has to be the way," Jake said. "Dad warned me enough times to stay away from here. And I found an old map at home. Dead Man's Cave is marked on it in dark red ink. We're going in the right direction . . . I know it."

Jake picked up the trail again on the far side of the clearing. He thought it was strange that the trail even still existed. After all, no one was supposed to come to Dead Man's Cave anymore.

Jake motioned Peter to hurry up and then set off down the narrow trail that twisted into a gully. Behind him, Peter was whimpering, "Jake, let's turn back."

"Go ahead, if you want," Jake answered. He knew Peter would never go back alone. He was too scared, and he was sure to get lost. The path was getting harder and harder to see now. Even Jake wasn't sure what direction they were going in anymore.

The trail leveled out in a heavily wooded forest at the bottom of the gully. The plants on the ground had changed from a bright green to a sickly greenish yellow. Toadstools grew around the thick tree trunks, some of them speckled with dark orange spots.

Jake looked up at the twisted branches of the dark trees overhead. They twined together like a spider's web over the path. There was a heavy, sickly sweet odor in the air, like the smell of something rotting, and strange insects crawled across the damp forest floor.

For the first time, Jake felt a current of fear pass through his body. He thought of the nightmares he'd had about Dead Man's Cave, ever since his parents had first told him about it. He wiped his hand across his forehead and noticed that his fingers were trembling. Before he could be tempted to turn back, he quickly walked through the trees toward a wall of brown and yellow ferns.

"Let's go home," Peter whimpered again from behind.

But it was too late. Just beyond the wall of ferns, Jake came to a sudden stop at the edge of a dark, deep hole. It was Dead Man's Cave, yawning down into the earth like an evil mouth. Jake felt Peter's cold fingers wrap around his arm.

"This is it," Jake whispered. He stared down into the deep pit that led to the mouth of the cave. There was something down there that he was determined to find. His father had told him about it. Something was just inside the cave that nobody had ever brought back. Jake didn't know what it was . . . but he planned to find out.

"Okay, we've seen it," Peter whispered. "Now let's get out of here." He tugged on Jake's arm and tried to pull him away from the edge.

"No, I'm going down," Jake said. "There's something I've got to get." He jerked his arm out of Peter's grip and grabbed hold of a bush that grew along the edge of the pit. Then he started climbing down toward Dead Man's Cave.

Peter leaned over the edge and yelled, "Get out!"

Deep, ghostly voices echoed back out of the pit,

GET OUT
    GET OUT
        GET OUT.

For a moment, Jake froze. He told himself that the voices had to be an echo. But they didn't sound like Peter. They sounded like the voices he'd heard in his nightmares. Jake looked up at Peter's face, peering over the edge of the pit. It was bleached white as a sheet.

"Go away!" Jake yelled at him angrily.

The voices breathed the words back at him, over and over,

GO AWAY
    GO AWAY
        GO AWAY.

Jake was too scared to move. Then something cold and slimy crawled over his hand. He looked down and saw a striped snake slither into a crack near his arm. With a scream, he jerked away his hand and fell down onto a ledge five feet below. Scrambling to his feet, he searched the rocks around him. He had never thought about snakes in Dead Man's Cave. Not even in his nightmares.

Another snake slithered across his foot. Jake jumped to the side and fell, twisting his leg under him. Painfully, he picked himself up and crept down toward the cave.

From the top of the pit, Peter shouted down another warning.

"Don't do it!"

Jake froze, waiting for the voices. This time, they screamed at him,

DON'T DO IT
    DON'T DO IT
        DON'T DO IT.

Jake was too close to turn back now. He ran

on toward the mouth of Dead Man's Cave with the echoing voices chasing after him. Finally, he reached the cave and fell on his knees in front of it. It was pitch-black inside, like an invisible curtain had been pulled down over it.

Jake reached out his hand into the cave. He felt cold air, like a dead man's breath, creep over his skin. He dropped his fingers to the cave floor, but all he felt was a squirming mass of baby snakes. Jake jerked away his hand in disgust; then, steeling his nerves, he searched the cave floor again. His fingers closed around something hard and cold. Trembling, he pulled it out into the light.

It was a skull — a human skull — covered with green mold. The eye sockets were empty holes and the yellow teeth were set in a weird grin. With a shudder, Jake held it up for Peter to see.

"It's mine," he yelled in triumph.

A strange silence hung over the pit. Jake looked around, waiting for the echoing voices.

"It's mine," he shouted again.

But Dead Man's Cave was as quiet as a tomb.

Jake looked back at the moldy skull sitting in his shaking hands. As he stared at it, the yellow teeth suddenly opened wide into a deathly grin. Then the skull whispered at Jake in a mocking voice, "No, it's mine!"

The last thing Jake heard was the skull's laughter echoing over and over against the walls of the pit. Then a ton of stones came crashing down, burying Jake forever in Dead Man's Cave.

The Midnight Feeding

The telephone frightened me when it first rang that night. I was all alone in the house, and I had just curled up with a book of ghost stories. My parents, you see, were away for the weekend. The ringing of the phone seemed like an intruder tapping at the window of my private little world.

I let the telephone ring five more times, trying to ignore it. I knew it couldn't be my parents, and I didn't feel like talking with anyone else. But the rings went on and on, jangling my nerves. Finally, I picked up the receiver and said, "Hello."

A woman whose voice I didn't recognize began talking very fast. She apologized for bothering me on such short notice and then said that she was desperate for a baby-sitter. She and her husband had recently moved into town, and they had just been invited to an important business dinner. She asked if I could please take care of their six-month-old son while they were gone.

When I hesitated to say yes, the woman quickly offered to pay me more than the usual fee. She said the dinner would last from 9:00 P.M. to 1:00 A.M., just four hours. And when she named the amount of money she was willing to pay, I didn't even think twice. I agreed to baby-sit immediately. The woman said she would be over to pick me up in twenty minutes and then quickly hung up the phone.

I looked down at my watch and saw that it was 8:30. That didn't give me much time to get ready. A nervous queasiness started in my stomach, and I suddenly wished that I had never agreed to take the job. It paid a lot of money, but everything had been so rushed and confused. Then I realized with a shock that I didn't even have the woman's address or telephone number. All I knew about her was her name, Mrs. Barloff.

I ran up to my room and pulled a warm sweater over my turtleneck and jeans. I kept getting the creepy feeling that I had made a mistake. But what could I do? I didn't have the woman's number to call her and cancel. And she would be showing up at my house in just a short time.

By 8:50, I was waiting at the front door. I had turned on the outside porch lights and put a house key in my jeans pocket. As I looked down the rainy street, I saw a big black car pull up to the curb. It waited there, its engine purring like a huge cat. For a few seconds, I wanted to run upstairs and hide in my bed. But I steeled my nerves and walked out the front door, locking it carefully behind me.

I ran through the drizzly rain out to the car and opened the front passenger's door. As the interior lights came on, I saw the driver. She had a very thin, pale face and long, thick, black hair. She curled her red lips into an artificial smile.

"I'm Mrs. Barloff. Thank you so much for helping us out tonight."

I said hello and stood in the rain by the open door, hesitating.

"Please get in," Mrs. Barloff said. "We don't have much time."

I slipped into the leather bucket seat and pulled the door shut. A second later, Mrs. Barloff took off down the street, accelerating to over the speed limit. I leaned back in the seat and nervously stared out the rain-streaked windshield.

"You will love our little Nicholas," she said with a slight accent that I hadn't noticed before. "He's only six months old, but already he's very intelligent."

"I look forward to meeting him," I said politely. "Is he still awake?"

"No, no, little Nicholas went to sleep an hour ago," she said. "But he'll wake up in time for his midnight feeding. Don't worry; he'll let you know when he's hungry."

I turned my eyes back to the dark road ahead of us and tried to relax. Maybe this night wouldn't be so bad after all. The baby would stay asleep until midnight, and I could read my book until then.

We drove on through the rain to the outskirts of town. The car tires squealed as Mrs. Barloff turned off the main road into a long, winding lane. I tried to figure out where we were, but I had lost my sense of direction in the dark night. Suddenly, we came around a curve and pulled up in front of a huge old house surrounded by towering fir trees. Two old-fashioned gas lamps burned in front of it, illuminating the front and throwing off strange, distorted shadows.

The house was painted a dark gray with yellow trim around the windows. The top floor was made up of strangely shaped gables, and the roof came to a high peak at the top like a witch's hat. I was sure that I had never seen this place before, because if I had, I never would have baby-sat there. My stomach was starting to feel sick, and I wished I could call my mom and dad to come pick me up.

Just then, my car door was pulled open, and I saw Mrs. Barloff standing by it, staring at me impatiently.

"Come along," she said tensely. "We really must hurry. My husband doesn't like to be late for dinner engagements."

Her voice had a commanding quality that made me obey her, even though I didn't want to. I followed her up the steps to the front door, which was made of heavy, carved oak. She put a large, black key in the lock and pushed it open.

We stepped into a narrow entrance hall that was dimly lit by real candles in wall sconces. They threw flickering shadows onto the dark walls that were covered with a black and red brocade paper. Mrs. Barloff flicked on an overhead chandelier when she saw the look of alarm on my face.

"Don't worry; you'll feel at home once you've

been here for awhile," she said, smiling nervously. "The baby's bedroom is on the second floor, and the kitchen is in the back of the house. You can settle down in the study through that door until Nicholas wakes up."

As she rattled off her instructions, I heard the sound of footsteps creaking on the staircase. Looking up, I saw a tall, thin man wearing a black tuxedo coming down the steps. In his lapel he wore a red carnation that contrasted with the unnaturally white pallor of his skin. As I met his intense gaze, I dropped my eyes to the floor. A terrible thought had crept into my mind. What if he was the one to take me home later that night?

"We must go now," Mrs. Barloff said the moment she saw her husband. "Remember to feed Nicholas at midnight. And, oh yes, one important thing. Do not open the curtains in his room."

She was gone before I could say anything more than good-bye. I heard the black car pull away down the drive. Then, suddenly, I realized I was alone in a strange house baby-sitting for a child that I'd never seen. I hurried to the front door and checked that it was locked tightly.

I started up the stairs to find the baby's room and to make certain that he was all right. I desperately hoped that he was still asleep so I could have three hours of peace and quiet before the midnight feeding. As I climbed the staircase, my heart began to beat faster. The hall ahead was dark and shadowy. I walked quickly to the end, where a door was slightly ajar. Softly, I pushed it open and peeked inside.

In the reddish glow of the nightlight, I saw a tall, wooden baby crib. Very quietly, I moved across the room toward the crib and bent over to look inside. A beautiful baby lay there with his face turned up to mine. He had perfect features crowned by a thick head of dark hair. Suddenly, as though he sensed my presence, Nicholas opened his eyes and stared at me for a long minute. I stood still, hypnotized by his gaze, until he closed his eyes again and went back to sleep. Still smiling from the sight of his sweet, innocent face, I walked back down the staircase. The Barloffs and their house gave me the creeps, but I loved baby Nicholas.

I picked up my bag and walked into the study that Mrs. Barloff had pointed to. The room was paneled in dark wood and filled with huge overstuffed chairs and two black leather couches. I sat down in a chair beside the only lamp that was turned on. It spread a pool of golden light around me but left most of the room in shadows.

I opened the bag to find my book of ghost stories and realized that I had left it at home in my rush to get ready. Frustrated, I stood up and walked over to a book-lined wall. I pulled out one book after another, but they were all in a foreign language that I didn't recognize.

Just then, a crack of thunder shook the air, followed by a jagged streak of lightning. I walked up to one of the red-curtained windows and pulled aside the heavy drapes. The fir trees outside were swaying in the wind, and rain was lashing down against the house. Suddenly, I wanted to talk to someone — my parents, my friends, anyone. I started to search the dark corners of the study for a telephone. It didn't make any sense, but I couldn't find one anywhere. I walked out into the hallway and looked, but none was there, either.

The feeling of desperation that had been lurking in my mind began to grow into panic. I ran across the hallway toward the dark living room. Stepping inside, I ran my hands along the wall, trying to find a light switch. Then suddenly I tripped over something that moved away into the darkness. I screamed and ran back into the study, huddling into the red chair under the pool of light. I curled my feet up under me and covered my face with my hands.

Then I started to cry in sobs that shook my body.

Wailing screams drifted in and out of my dreams until I suddenly woke up and looked around in panic. For a second, I didn't know where I was. Then it all came back to me in a rush. I was at the Barloff's house, and I had fallen asleep in the study. The screams were coming from upstairs, where poor little Nicholas was crying for his midnight feeding.

I looked at my watch and saw that it was 12:15. How long had the baby been crying before I woke up? I jumped up and ran through the hallway back to the dark kitchen, listening to his screams echo through the house.

As I flicked on the light in the kitchen, I saw a large mouse — or was it a rat? — scurry across the floor and hide under a cabinet near the refrigerator. Quickly, I ran to the refrigerator and pulled open the door. One baby bottle filled with dark juice sat on the top shelf. I searched everywhere for another bottle filled with milk but couldn't find one. Finally, I picked up the juice bottle, ran for the staircase, and pounded up the steps with my heart in my throat.

As I walked into Nicholas's room, I saw his silhouette standing up against the bars of the crib. The moment he saw me, he stopped crying and reached out his arms for the bottle. I gave it to him and watched as he took long, deep drinks of the dark juice. A rush of relief flooded through my body. The baby was all right; he had just been screaming from hunger. I searched the room for a lamp or wall switch so I could see Nicholas better. Finally I walked over to the windows that were covered with heavy drapes. I remembered Mrs. Barloff's warning not to open them. But she must have meant before the feeding, in case the light would wake Nicholas. I reached up and pulled back the drapes from the window behind the crib.

Looking out at the sky, I saw that the clouds had cleared away after the storm, and a full moon was shining in the sky. Its silvery light shone down on Nicholas standing in his crib. The baby turned around with the bottle in his mouth and stared up at the moon.

Then I heard a strange thumping sound on the window just behind Nicholas's head. I walked closer and saw the shape of a bat's body pressed against the glass, peering in at the baby. As I shrank back in disgust, a second bat landed on the glass. The baby seemed fascinated by their weird, humanlike faces staring at him in the moonlight. He suddenly threw his bottle out of the crib onto the floor and leaned closer to the window. I walked over to where the bottle had fallen and picked it up. There were only a few drops of the thick, dark juice left, and I noticed that the nipple had four tiny holes in it.

Just then, Nicholas turned around to stare at me and began to cry in long, loud sobs. He reached his arms out to be picked up. I bent over his crib and took him in my arms. Immediately, he stopped crying and clung to my neck.

Behind me, I heard another bat land on the window with a thump. I saw Nicholas's shining eyes staring at them in the light of the full moon. Then I lifted him up to my shoulder to pat his back. As I drew his head near my neck, I felt his soft body go suddenly rigid. A strange hiss came from his mouth into my ear.

And, just as I finally understood, I felt his four tiny fangs sinking into my neck.

When Darkness Comes

The light from the small antique shop shone out onto the dark, rain-drenched street. Walking by, Matthew Cooper found himself drawn to the light like a moth winging through a black sky. He shivered as the cold November wind cut through his trenchcoat; then, almost without thinking, he pulled down his dripping umbrella in front of the shop's door.

A small brass bell tinkled as Matthew pushed open the door and stepped inside. The smell of musty old books and a faint odor of incense filled the room. Matthew glanced quickly around but couldn't find a shopkeeper anywhere. Uneasily, he began to walk around the room, examining its marble statues, antique tables, and mementos from the past. He felt uncomfortable about being alone in the shop, yet he was too intrigued to leave.

Matthew walked over to a round oak table covered by cast-iron figures of famous people. He ran his fingers over the cold features of Napoleon, George Washington, and Queen Victoria. Then he turned away from them to study a bookshelf lined with leather-bound volumes. He read row after row of titles, all about witchcraft, ghosts, and stories of horror. Matthew felt a shudder creep over his body and wondered again where the shopkeeper might be.

He turned his eyes away from the bookshelf to a corner of the room where a painting hung in the shadow of a tall Chinese vase. Immediately, his imagination was drawn to it. He walked nearer and moved the vase aside for a better view.

The old oil painting was hung in an ornate frame of carved wood and gilt. The picture was of a castle sitting on top of a tree-covered hill. The night sky was lit by a hazy moon that hovered near the castle. But what caught Matthew's attention most was a small window cut into the highest tower. A golden light shone from it, piercing the darkness around it.

Matthew suddenly jumped as the sound of a cough came from over his shoulder. He whirled around to face a withered old woman who stared at him with sharp blue eyes.

"An unusual picture," she said, looking from

Matthew to the dark painting. "I'll let you have it for a good price."

An hour later, Matthew leaned over the table in his study, where he had laid down the painting. With trembling hands, he tore away the brown paper that the old shopkeeper had wrapped it in. Matthew worried that the painting might disappoint him outside the cluttered surroundings of the antique store. But he was not disappointed. Lifting up the painting, Matthew hung it on the wall across from his desk. Then, once again, he stared at the mysterious light in the tower window, wondering why it shone.

His friends were never sure if Matthew lived alone because of his strange habits or if he had strange habits because he lived alone. Now they added the old painting to his eccentric ways. Matthew seemed to talk of little else. He was convinced that he had made a rare and valuable find. He seemed obsessed by the meaning of the lighted window in the castle tower. When his friends asked to see the painting, he promised to show it to them as soon as it had been cleaned by a fine restorer of old art.

Matthew arranged to pick up the painting from the restorer late one afternoon. He had invited his friends to the house to see it that night, and he nervously worried that the painting might not be finished.

But when the gray-haired restorer answered his doorbell that afternoon, he assured Matthew that the painting had been cleaned beautifully. The man led him into the back of the shop, where Matthew saw his painting lying alone on a large worktable. Its surface seemed to have been stripped of a layer of dust and grime, and all its details were plain to see.

Matthew could see the golden light shining from the tower even brighter than before. He saw a decorated crest over the castle door. And in the thick trees at the bottom of the castle, he saw the yellow eyes of animals hiding in the night. Then, for the first time, Matthew saw a line of words painted in the bottom right corner of the picture. They were in Latin. Slowly, Matthew translated their meaning.

"Every century, darkness comes," he said, turning to the old man. "What could it mean?"

"The painting has a story, you know," the old man said, breaking into Matthew's thoughts.

Matthew stared at the man in surprise. "Do you mean you've seen this painting before?"

"No . . . but I've heard of it," the man answered. "It's a rather famous painting, in its own way. The picture is of an old castle in Scotland. Many centuries ago, legend has it, a young lord died mysteriously in that highest tower. No one knows if it was murder, but they say there is still a curse on the castle. And, some believe, the same curse is carried by this painting."

"But the words," Matthew said. "What do they mean?"

The old man shrugged and began to say something. Then, suddenly, he looked at the picture and broke off his story. He hastily began to wrap the picture for Matthew to take home.

"Finish your story, please," Matthew asked him. But the old man shook his head and nervously hurried Matthew out of the shop.

Matthew took the painting home and hung it back on his wall. But he couldn't get the old man's story out of his mind. If the painting was so famous, why had he been able to buy it for so little money? And what did the man mean by a curse?

Matthew was so preoccupied with the painting that he was surprised to hear his doorbell ring. When he opened the door and saw his friends standing there, he had to ask them to help prepare their own dinner. Later, when the meal was over, Matthew's friends insisted on seeing the painting he had talked about so often.

Matthew led them up the stairs to his third-floor study, where the painting hung. On the way, his friends all laughed and joked about the light in the tower and what it could mean. Matthew forced himself to laugh with them, but he couldn't get the old man's story out of his mind.

At the top of the stairs, Matthew threw open the door to his study, flicked on the light switch, and led his friends over to the wall where the painting hung. Immediately, his eyes turned to the highest tower of the castle. It was dark. The glowing light that had shone there was gone.

Behind him, Matthew heard embarrassed laughter. His friends came closer to the painting, trying to find the lighted tower. He turned around to face them, insisting that the light had been there, even after the painting was cleaned.

One of his friends leaned closer to the painting and read the Latin words at its bottom.

"Every century, darkness comes," he said. Then he added with a hollow laugh, "This must be the night."

Matthew felt a cold sweat break out over his body. He wanted his friends to leave. He was tired of their mocking laughter. And, suddenly, he was obsessed by a desire to call the old man and learn the end of his story.

Matthew hurried his friends out of the study and down the stairs. He told them that he needed a good night's sleep. They left the house soon after, whispering to each other and staring at him. As soon as he was alone in the house, Matthew went to the telephone and rang the number of the old man who had restored the painting. He could hear the phone ring far away, over and over, but no one answered.

Matthew hadn't planned to go back up to his study to see the painting again, but a compelling curiosity came over him. He wondered if the light in the tower was still out. He wondered if, somehow, his friends had tricked him. Trying to calm his pounding heart, Matthew climbed back up the stairs to find out.

With shaking hands, he turned the doorknob and walked inside the study. The painting hung on the far wall, full of dark shadows. There was no light in the tower window. Darkness had come over the castle. Matthew walked up to the painting and stared at the tower window that used to glow with light. What terrible thing was happening in that small, dark room?

Fingers of fear crept around Matthew's mind

and tightened their grip on him. He thought he heard the sound of footsteps coming up the stairs toward him. But, just as he pulled his eyes away from the dark painting, the light in his study suddenly flickered and went out. And then, out of the night, darkness came for Matthew Cooper.

The next morning, two of his friends found Matthew's body sprawled on the floor in front of the painting. And, strangest of all, a light was shining from the highest tower in the castle, shining right down on Matthew's dead body.

King of the Cats

The old gravedigger leaned against his shovel and stared up at the dark sky. The moon was nothing more than a thin sickle hanging over the graveyard. Not one silvery star shone against the black blanket of the night.

The gravedigger muttered to himself and picked up his shovel again. He thrust it down into the hard, cold earth. Shovelful by shovelful, he dug out Mrs. Witherspoon's grave. She had died without warning that morning. And without warning, her family had decided to bury her the next day. They had given the old gravedigger a few extra dollars to dig the grave at night. He'd taken the money, but it didn't make him happy.

The truth was, he didn't like the graveyard at night. During the day, it was different. The sun shone down on the tombstones. Visitors brought flowers and put them on the graves. The gravedigger felt part of the living even as he dug holes for the dead.

But at night, the graveyard belonged only to the dead. Skeletons lay in their coffins under the green grass. The tombstones hunched in the dark like ghostly shadows. And the very earth was harder and colder.

The gravedigger stuck his shovel into the high mound of dirt piled along one side of the grave. He picked up his old lantern and carried it around to the other side. Its flickering light cast shadows on the nearby tombstones of Mrs. Witherspoon's relatives. As the gravedigger set the lantern down, he heard a strange sound echo through the tombstones in the cemetery. It was the meow of a cat. It reminded him of Old Tom, his black cat at home. Old Tom was probably stretched out in front of the fireplace right now.

The gravedigger thought about the warm fire and his wife sitting in front of it, knitting. He cursed Mrs. Witherspoon for dying this morning. Then he fell to work, digging her grave faster and faster. After ten shovelfuls of dirt, he stopped to catch his breath. Once again, he heard the strange meow echo through the tombstones. It was louder this time, as though it came from a very big cat.

The gravedigger felt a chill at the back of his neck and pulled up his jacket collar. He had dug graves at night before. And each time this happened. Some sound would frighten him and bring on the shivers. He started shoveling furiously, wanting to get the grave dug and done with. Then he would go home, sit down by the fire, and pet Old Tom's glossy black fur.

His shovel hit a large stone five feet down in the earth. The gravedigger cursed and bent down to work out the stone. He was kneeling in the grave, out of sight, when the meowing sound came again. This time it was so close that it made the gravedigger jump.

Slowly, he lifted up his head to peer out of the grave. The sight he saw made his blood run as cold as the corpses around him.

Nine black cats were marching toward the grave upright on their hind legs. Eight were carrying a coffin on their shoulders, four on each side. The coffin was just three feet long and was covered by a red velvet pall. On top of it sat a small golden crown that shone as bright as the cats' yellow eyes.

In front of the coffin, leading the others, was the biggest cat of all. He carried a lantern held high in his right paw. The gravedigger saw that the cat's right paw had a spot of white on it, just like Old Tom's. Then he noticed that all the cats had a white spot on their right paws, like a special mark.

The cats marched in perfect time with each other. Every fourth step they said, "Meow."

The gravedigger quickly reached out for his lantern and snuffed out the light. Then he crouched down in the grave, shaking with fear. He had seen strange things before in the cemetery at night. But he had never seen anything so strange as these nine black cats and their coffin.

The gravedigger huddled against the cold ground of the grave, hoping the cats would pass him by. But the next meow was even closer yet. He sat as still as a corpse in a coffin. But the next meow was even closer yet.

Then the light of a lantern fell across the piles of dirt beside the grave. The light grew stronger and stronger. Finally, it shone down into the hole of Mrs. Witherspoon's grave.

The gravedigger raised his fearful eyes and looked up. The biggest cat was standing over the grave, holding its lantern. Its big yellow eyes stared down at the gravedigger. Then the cat opened his mouth wide and began to talk.

"Tell Tom Tildrum that Tim Toldrum has died."

The gravedigger jumped bolt upright in the

grave. He stared the black cat straight in the eyes.

"Tell Tom Tildrum that Tim Toldrum has died," the cat said again.

The gravedigger scrambled out of the grave he'd dug and took a final look at the nine black cats and their coffin. Then he screamed and ran past them out of the cemetery. He didn't stop running until he reached the door of his house. He threw it open, ran inside, and then bolted the door behind him.

His wife looked up from her rocking chair by the fireplace.

The gravedigger rushed over to her and asked in a trembling voice, "Who's Tom Tildrum?"

Old Tom jumped up from his rug by the fireplace and let out a loud meow.

The gravedigger's wife led him to a chair by the fire and sat him down.

"Who's Tom Tildrum?" he asked again, his eyes gleaming like a madman's.

Old Tom jumped up, putting his right paw on the gravedigger's knee. Its white spot gleamed in the firelight.

The gravedigger's wife brought him a blanket and a mug of warm milk. But still he kept asking, over and over, "Who's Tom Tildrum?"

Old Tom started pacing and meowing in front of the fire, his yellow eyes fixed on the gravedigger.

The gravedigger started shivering again in spite of the warm blanket and milk. He couldn't forget about the black cats with Old Tom prowling back and forth in front of him.

"What about Tom Tildrum?" his wife finally asked.

Carefully, the gravedigger repeated the big cat's words.

"Tell Tom Tildrum that Tim Toldrum is dead."

As the words came out of the gravedigger's mouth, Old Tom arched his back and bared his teeth. Then he stood upright on his two hind legs.

"Tim Toldrum's dead!" he cried. "Then I — Tom Tildrum — am King of the Cats!"

With a switch of his black tail, Old Tom jumped up the chimney . . . and was never seen again.

The White Dove

The night fell like a heavy blanket over the white-pillared house of Wesley Reynolds. Inside, servants moved in silence up and down the great stairs and in and out of the bedroom where Mrs. Reynolds lay dying. The room was full of the sickly sweet smell of magnolias, her favorite flower. Mrs. Reynolds lay on a canopy bed, her head propped up on lace pillows. By her bedside, Wesley leaned over and wiped her fevered brow. His wife's burning eyes and sunken cheeks told him that the end was near.

"Wesley," he heard her whisper through parched lips. "Promise me something."

Choking back his tears, Wesley nodded his head and bent nearer to his beloved wife to hear her dying wish.

"Never marry again, Wesley," she said in a soft, insistent whisper. "Promise me."

Wesley would have promised her anything at this moment. He vowed to her that he would never marry again, although he was still a young man.

"You must not worry about being lonely," his wife said between gasping breaths. "I will come back to keep you company. Watch for me in the garden. I will come back to you as a white dove."

With those words, she died.

Long after the funeral was over, the great house remained a place of mourning. Only when a young servant forgot herself did laughter ring out in the rooms. Wesley Reynolds wore black for a year, and even after that, he seemed to wear a black band around his heart. He had loved his wife very much, and her dying words seemed to work on him like a curse. He acted as though he, too, had given up life.

Every day, no matter what the weather, he went out into the beautiful garden that lay beyond the back patio of the house. He would sit there for hours, staring into the trees and high bushes. The servants and his friends knew what he was watching for. But a white dove never came.

* * *

At last, five years after his wife's death, Wesley met a young woman who woke him from his mournful trance. In her sparkling eyes and playful smile, he found life again. He forgot the deathbed vow he had made to his wife. He wanted his lonely life to be filled with the laughter and love of this beautiful young woman. They set their wedding date for just three months later.

The night before the wedding was cold and damp. Wesley was preparing to go to sleep in the bedroom he had shared with his old wife and would soon share with his new. He swung open the windows for fresh air but suddenly found himself chilled. As he went to pull the windows shut, he caught a glimpse of the moonlight shining on a white form perched on a nearby windowsill. The sight made his heart tighten in his chest. Then he heard the soft, insistent cooing of a dove.

Wesley slammed the windows shut with trembling hands. Then, to his horror, he saw the white dove fly up off its perch and settle on the windowsill inches away from his eyes. Its cooing was louder and louder now. He pulled shut the heavy curtains over the window and doused the light on his bedstand. Trembling, he slipped into bed and pulled the blankets up over his shivering body.

Then, through the dark silence of the room, he heard the dove's wings flapping desperately against the windowpane. He heard its beak peck, peck, peck against the glass. And all through the night, the dove's eerie call haunted his troubled dreams.

At the wedding the next day, all the guests remarked on the bride's beauty and the groom's terrible pallor. Wesley Reynolds seemed to have aged ten years overnight, people said. There were whispers among those who knew of his vow to his dying wife. Her memory seemed to hang over the wedding like a dark shadow.

After the ceremony, Wesley and his new wife ran down the church steps through a shower of rice and rose petals. The couple smiled and shared another kiss as they walked toward the horse and carriage that would carry them to the wedding reception. But as Wesley went to lift his bride into the carriage, he suddenly shrank back in terror. A white dove was sitting on the seat, staring at him with its black, beady eyes.

His bride saw it and laughed; then she tried to shoo it away with a brush of her hand. A second later, she drew her hand back with a scream. Blood was rushing from the small hole that the dove had pecked near her wedding ring. In a trembling voice, Welsey ordered the carriage driver to frighten away the bird; then he wrapped his bride's hand in her lace wedding handkerchief.

The wedding dinner was held in the garden of the Reynolds' mansion. Tables were set up under the old trees hung with Spanish moss. But Wesley seemed to forget the happiness of the occasion as he searched the branches of the trees above his bride, over and over again.

The new Mr. and Mrs. Reynolds left the wedding reception much earlier than the guests thought was proper. And the servants noticed that, after the couple left, the strange white dove that had cooed all during the meal left the garden, too.

The newly married couple did not return from their honeymoon abroad until six months later. They had wandered from place to place, from hotel to hotel, trying to forget their wedding day. At last, Wesley had to return home to his business. Reluctantly, he and his wife came back to live in the old, white-pillared house.

On their first morning at the house, Wesley and his wife rose late, and after breakfast, strolled outside to admire the spring flowers in the garden. After walking around the long oval path that wound through the trees and shrubs, they sat down on a wooden bench near a small pond. They began to talk of plans for their new life together. Then, suddenly, Wesley stopped speaking. He had heard a sound behind him, a low, weird sound that sent shivers down his spine. When he looked into his wife's eyes, clouded with fear, he knew that she had heard it, too.

As they sat together in silence, they heard the flapping of wings come closer and closer. They turned around just as the white dove landed on the back of the bench. It stared at them with beady, accusing eyes and began to coo its dreadful song.

Quickly, the young wife hid her hands in her skirts and ran back into the house, sobbing uncontrollably. For a long while, Wesley sat looking at the dove, returning its stare of dark hatred. Then he, too, went inside to escape the bird's insane cooing that echoed over and over in his brain.

By day, the white dove haunted the garden, making Wesley and his wife prisoners inside the house. By night, it perched on the windowsill outside their bedroom, disturbing their sleep. Slowly, the house fell back into its state of mourning. The servants whispered that the white dove was the first Mrs. Reynolds, come back to haunt her husband for breaking his vow to her as she lay on her deathbed. They were all afraid of the dove and refused to chase it away when Wesley ordered them to.

As the weeks wore on, Wesley could see that his new marriage was doomed. His wife grew pale and nervous. She began to tremble each time the dove appeared and began its song. Finally, she begged to go back to her father's house. One afternoon, Wesley sent her off in a carriage, watching his happiness fade away in the distance.

By the next morning, Wesley had made up his mind. In the still light of dawn, he dressed and went to the cabinet where his guns were kept. He chose a rifle and loaded it with birdshot. Then he crept into the garden and waited. At last, the white dove winged into the garden and landed on a rosebush. The bird did not notice him hiding only yards away.

Wesley raised the rifle and pulled the trigger. Seconds later, a woman's angry scream rose from the throat of the dove; then red blood spread across its white breast feathers. To Wesley's horror, the bird did not fall dead; it flew away into the sky with a terrifying shriek.

That night, Wesley did not sleep. Hour after hour, he listened in terror to the peck, peck, peck of the dove's beak on his windowpane.

Just before dawn, he heard the glass break at last.

The next morning, his servants found him dead. They buried him on the hillside next to his first wife. And it is said that a white dove still visits the graves, cooing its mad song.

Cemetery Hill

We met on a dark corner by the cemetery that Halloween night — Rick, Jimmy, and me. Kids dressed up in costumes were still out trick-or-treating all over town. But none of them walked by that corner. The cemetery was right behind us, and the white tombstones loomed up out of the dark like ghosts in the moonlight. I had chosen it as a meeting place because I knew we would be all alone.

As soon as Rick saw me, he asked nervously, "Did you bring it?"

"Sure," I answered. "It's right here in my pocket."

"Let me see it," Jimmy asked eagerly, looking around to check that nobody was watching.

I reached into my pocket and pulled out the coil of wire. It was a special kind that my father uses in his work — very thin and very strong.

I let Jimmy take a closer look at it and then grabbed it away from him and put it back in my pocket. This prank had been my idea, and I wanted to stay in charge.

"Okay, I think we're ready," I said. "I can't wait to hear the first person scream."

Rick and Jimmy started to laugh, but their laughter sounded sort of hollow, as though they didn't really mean it.

"Are you sure we should go through with this?" Rick asked nervously. "What if . . ."

"What's the matter with you?" I demanded. "This is Halloween night. We're out here to scare people. If you can't take it, go home and pass out candy."

I didn't wait for Rick to answer. I turned and started on the footpath that goes up Cemetery Hill. A few minutes later, I heard the two of them running to catch up with me.

We walked three across up the path to the top of the hill. The little kids we passed all bunched together and got out of our way. We were dressed all in black, and I guess that we looked scary — like creatures of the night.

I had chosen Cemetery Hill as the best place to play the prank. The path that goes up the hill is lined on both sides by big, old trees. At the top you can look down and see the town on one side. On the other side is the highway that leads out of the city.

Most of the people who commute by bus from our town have to walk up Cemetery Hill to get to their houses on the other side. And tonight we'd be waiting for them.

When we reached the top of the hill, I pulled out the coil of wire and handed one end of it to Rick.

"You two take this across the path and climb up in that big tree on the other side," I ordered them.

I felt the wire unraveling as they walked across the path. Then I grabbed hold of my end and climbed up a tree that was directly across from theirs. The wire was so sharp that it cut into my hands, and I pulled off a twig to wrap it around.

We had only been up in the trees for about five minutes when I looked down Cemetery Hill and saw our first victim. He was walking up the hill, carrying a briefcase and wearing a nice high hat.

I gave the wire a jerk to get Rick and Jimmy's attention. I could see them like dark shadows in the tree across the footpath.

As the man came closer and closer to us, I

reached my arm down to lower the wire over the path. Rick did the same thing on the other side.

The man came walking toward us, not suspecting a thing. Then, all of a sudden, his hat flew right off his head. In the moonlight, we could see the look of fear come over his face. He looked as scared as a little kid, then he took off running.

As soon as he was out of earshot, we all cracked up laughing. The prank was working even better than we had planned. On other Halloween nights, we'd scared kids; but scaring adults was a lot better.

We did the same thing to four more men during the next hour. They would all come walking up the hill, whistling or humming to themselves. Then, as soon as they got close, we'd dip the wire down and flip off their hats. They all looked as though they'd seen a ghost; one even started screaming as he ran down the hill.

I was having a good time and couldn't wait for our next victim to walk by. But Jimmy yelled at me from across the path that he and Rick wanted to go home. They said their hands were beginning to freeze.

I tried to talk them into staying, but they

kept arguing with me. Then I looked down Cemetery Hill and saw a man getting off the bus at the bottom.

"Just one more," I called over to Rick and Jimmy. "We'll get this guy good. Then we can go home."

The man who was coming up the hill toward us seemed taller than the rest of our victims. He was carrying a suitcase in each hand and had on the kind of hat that Sherlock Holmes wore. He seemed to be walking fast, but I guess that was because of his long legs.

I gave the wire another tug to make sure it was good and tight. The man was only a few yards away now. I tried to judge exactly how low I should drop the wire; it was hard to figure out because this man seemed to get taller and taller the closer he came.

We got ready and started to lower the wire over the path. Then, just when the man was a few feet away, a cloud moved over the bright moon. A second later, the sky was pitch-black. All of a sudden, I felt a sickening pull on the wire. It almost jerked me right out of the tree, but I grabbed hold of a branch. Then, from below, I heard a choked scream, followed by the plop of something heavy hitting the ground.

Then, as the moon came out from behind the

cloud, I looked down at the path below me. I saw the man's head lying there with its eyes staring up at me. And then the bloody head started to roll, over and over, down Cemetery Hill.

Claustrophobia

Derek stood outside the door to his aunt's sitting room, nervously pulling at the stiff white collar around his neck. He felt his lungs growing tight and his breath coming in painful, shallow gasps. He always felt like this when he went in to see Aunt Edith in her small, dark sitting room. Even outside the door, in the spacious hallway, he felt the panicky sense of claustrophobia overwhelm him.

A bell rang shrilly from inside the room. It was Aunt Edith's signal that she was ready to see him. She had grown too old and too obese to get up from her chair and welcome in people herself. Derek noticed that he was grinding his teeth as he turned the doorknob; with a great effort, he set his lips in an artificial smile and walked into the room.

As always, Derek was shocked to see how

small the room was. The far wall was so narrow that a brick fireplace completely filled it up. Aunt Edith sat in front of the fireplace in a huge, red velvet chair, staring at him with her heavy-lidded eyes. Dark drapes hung over the two windows to the outside, shutting out the sunlight.

"Don't just stand there, Derek," Aunt Edith said. "Shut the door and come in."

Hesitantly, Derek closed the door behind him, shutting off his only means of escape. Aunt Edith motioned for him to take a seat in one of the overstuffed chairs facing hers. When he didn't move, she pointed a fat finger at him and then at the chair. Derek stumbled toward the chair and sank down into its deep cushions, unable to look anywhere but straight ahead at Aunt Edith's bloated face.

"You must be curious, Derek, about why I called you here today," she began.

Derek nodded his head at her but didn't say a word. In fact, he seldom spoke during their interviews. He'd learned years ago, when he was just a little boy, that Aunt Edith didn't want conversation. She just wanted an audience.

"I learned yesterday that I'm going to die soon," Aunt Edith said in a cold, matter-of-fact voice. She continued to stare at him without a flicker of emotion on her face.

Derek struggled to find something appropriate to say. He was shocked and disturbed by her news. But his tongue had gone thick, and his mind was fighting off the desire to bolt from the room and run outside.

Aunt Edith watched him squirm in the chair like a trapped animal. A mocking smile creased her face into ridges of fat.

"I thought I might see a glimmer of delight on your face," she said, pinning him down with her gaze. "But you simply look like a frightened rabbit, as you always do."

"I'm sorry, Aunt Edith," Derek finally stammered. "Very sorry."

"I'm sure you are, Derek," she quickly answered with sarcastic malice. "Well, I need you to do me a favor, Derek, before death comes knocking on my door. That's why I asked you here today."

Derek stared intently at the fireplace behind Aunt Edith. He knew if he concentrated on it very hard, he could keep the claustrophobia from driving him mad. It was strange, he suddenly realized, that in all the years he had sat before the fireplace, there had never — ever — been a fire in it.

"Why are you staring at that fireplace, Derek?" Aunt Edith demanded. "I've watched you doing it for years, and I've always wondered if you knew my secret."

Derek turned his eyes away from the fireplace to stare at his aunt's face. What secret was she talking about? For years, he had kept his claustrophobia a secret from her. He had never trusted what Aunt Edith might do to him if she knew.

"That fireplace has hidden my secret for twenty years now," Aunt Edith said in a low voice. "Only your Uncle Peter and I have ever known about it." She paused and ran her eyes up and down Derek's body from his head to his toes.

"You must be wondering why I'm telling you about this, Derek. Well, I thought of you because you're so like your Uncle Peter," she said. "Like you, he was tall and very, very thin. Actually, skinny. I never did like skinny men."

Derek watched in disgust as she laughed at her own words.

"Of course, skinny men have their uses," Aunt Edith went on. "Your Uncle Peter hid my secret in the fireplace just before he died. And now, you're going to get it out. Come here, Derek, come here."

Aunt Edith motioned to him impatiently.

Derek pulled himself out of the overstuffed chair and walked the few steps it took to stand in front of his aunt. The smell of her heavy, expensive perfume filled the air, making him dizzy and weak-kneed. He felt the walls of the room begin to close in around him.

"Listen," Aunt Edith said in an even lower voice, almost a whisper. "There is a box hidden high inside the fireplace. No one else alive, no one but the two of us, knows that it is there."

Derek found himself hanging on every word. His mind was racing with thoughts about what might be in the box. Perhaps, he hoped wildly, Aunt Edith was finally going to reward him for all the time he had sat in her small, stuffy sitting room.

"Of course, your Uncle Peter knew what was in the box," Aunt Edith went on. "He was so very angry with me about what I had done. He never even let me wear the diamonds before he hid them away."

Derek felt his hands begin to tremble and his heart begin to beat faster. Edith suddenly paused and searched his face with her cold, piercing eyes.

"I see Peter was right. He told me people become too curious about diamonds. Well, it doesn't matter now. I will be dead soon, and no one can send me to jail for stealing them."

As she saw the expression of surprise come over Derek's face, Aunt Edith broke into a strange, cackling laughter.

"You're shocked, aren't you, my little rabbit? You'd never have the courage to steal anything, would you? I used to be quite good at it until your Uncle Peter caught me. I would go into jewelry stores that trusted me as a valued customer. Without them even suspecting, I would steal their diamonds. Oh, how I loved to hide away those hard, shiny stones in secret places."

Derek shrank back as Edith once again threw back her head and roared with laughter, her rolls of fat shaking obscenely.

"Now, let's talk about how you can help me, Derek," Aunt Edith said, her voice full of ice again. "Your Uncle Peter cut a hole into the fireplace flue fifteen feet up from the ground. He hid the box holding the diamonds in that space. All you have to do is crawl up and get the box. And you needn't worry about soot or ashes. I've never used the fireplace for all these years, just in case I might harm the diamonds."

Derek felt fear rise like a dark tide in his mind as he looked into the narrow opening of the fireplace. How could he ever fit inside it?

"I remember exactly how your Uncle Peter

did it," Aunt Edith said, seeming to read his thoughts. "Once you crawl into the hearth, you can stand up and just fit inside the flue. Peter pounded iron footholds into the sides of the chimney every two feet up. All you have to do is climb up them until you feel the hole where the box of diamonds is hidden."

Edith paused, staring at Derek's white, sweating face. "Don't look like such a coward, Derek. You'll either do this for me or I'll find some way to make you. Surely you don't think I'm going to let you walk out of here without getting the diamonds, now that you know my secret."

Without thinking, Derek made a sudden lunge for the door. But Aunt Edith heaved up from her chair and blocked his escape. She waddled over to the door, turned the key, and then hid it in the folds of her dress.

"The sooner you do what I say, Derek, the better things will go for you in the future," she said in a cold, demanding voice.

Derek began to tremble inside. He had always feared Aunt Edith, but not like this. She came toward him, pressing him closer and closer to the fireplace. He crouched down and found himself crawling to safety into the opening of the hearth.

"That's right, Derek," Aunt Edith ordered. "Now stand up inside the flue and start to climb."

Derek followed her orders, his mind dizzy with fear. He sucked the thick, dusty air into his lungs and struggled to find the first foothold. Then he pushed his body upwards, climbing onto one foothold after another. Suddenly the walls of the flue seemed to be closing in around him like a brick coffin. Derek panicked and started to scramble back down to the bottom, where a dim shaft of light glowed.

Suddenly, the light was blotted out, and Aunt Edith's voice echoed up the flue. "Don't try to come down without the diamonds, Derek," she hissed. "I won't let you out."

Derek began to climb back up again, but the walls seemed even tighter now. He went higher and higher, and just when he thought he would go mad, he felt an opening in the bricks. Groping around in the dark, his fingers closed around a moldy velvet box. Derek clutched it and quickly slid back down the flue.

"I have it," he whimpered into the sealed-off entrance of the fireplace. "Aunt Edith, let me out."

With a snort of triumph, Edith pulled away the chair she had blocked the fireplace with. Then she bent down and grabbed the box from

Derek's scraped and bleeding hands.

Crouched there in that small, dark place, Derek stared at her greedy, bloated face. And he vowed revenge.

Three weeks later, Aunt Edith died. She left precise instructions for the undertaker to follow regarding her funeral. The coffin was the best available, made of heavy mahogany with a thick lead liner. Edith was laid out in an expensive midnight blue dress. And on her fingers and arms and neck and ears were diamonds, an extravagant wealth of diamonds. The body was put on view in Edith's sitting room, just as she had requested.

All the other relatives gasped when they saw the jewels sparkling on Edith's corpse. Only Derek stared at her body in the coffin with silent hatred. He had learned about her will that morning. Aunt Edith had left him the furniture in her sitting room. That was all. The will stated that the diamonds were to remain on her body and be buried with her. They twinkled up at Derek like laughing eyes as he stared down at Edith's body in the coffin.

The night before the burial, Derek paced back and forth in the hallway outside the sitting room where Edith lay. He had been instructed by the undertaker to wait until the last visitor left and then close up the coffin. The hearse would come to take away Aunt Edith's body at 11:00.

Impatiently, Derek watched one relative after another go in and out of the room, gossiping about the diamonds and Aunt Edith. Finally, at 10:45, Derek closed the front door on the last visitor. He didn't have much time. But he was determined to get his reward for what Aunt Edith had done to him.

Derek walked into the small sitting room that was almost filled by Edith's massive coffin. He walked up to it and leaned over her dead body. Quickly, one by one, he ripped the diamond bracelets from her swollen wrists. Then, with a cry of triumph, he pulled off the necklace and earrings.

Derek left the rings for last. The thought of picking up her hands to pull them off disgusted him. But the huge, sparkling diamonds were too tempting to leave. Derek forced himself to grasp her right hand and tried to twist off the biggest diamond from her middle finger. But the diamond wouldn't budge.

The sickly sweet smell of Aunt Edith's perfume drifted into Derek's nostrils and made him feel faint. In panic, he looked around the walls of the sitting room. They seemed to be moving closer and closer around him. He wiped his sweating brow and, again, tried to remove the ring. But it was stuck on Aunt Edith's finger as though it were part of her body.

Just then, Derek heard the sound of the hearse pulling up in front of the house. He knew he didn't have much time left, but he couldn't leave that ring behind. Climbing up on the steps in front of the coffin, Derek swung one leg inside and took hold of the ring with both hands.

Then, suddenly, Aunt Edith's cold, stiff fingers began to curl around his hands. They crawled up his arms and, with the strong grip of death, pulled him down beside her into the coffin.

The last thing Derek saw was Aunt Edith's dead blue lips curl into a sneer. Then the coffin lid slammed shut on him . . . forever.

Island of Fear

The six scouts stood by the edge of the lake and looked out at the small islands that dotted its wide waters. The boys had been camping together at the lake for three weeks. Tonight, they would face their final survival test.

"Think you're ready, Ty?" Phil asked in a mocking voice.

"Sure," Ty answered, his voice cracking to a high squeak. "I know how to start a fire and put up camp and all that."

"I hear that camping skills aren't the problem," Eric said, staring out across the water. "It's the loneliness that gets to you. And what happens to your imagination."

Ty looked nervously from Phil to Eric through his thick-lensed glasses. He knew that they were probably just trying to scare him. They were always giving him a hard time because he was the youngest and smallest scout in the troop.

"Come on, you guys," Mark interrupted. "All we have to do is spend one night alone on an island. Big deal."

"And we even have emergency flares in case we get in trouble," Brad said. "What can happen to us out here?"

Eric hadn't taken his eyes off the islands in the lake. "I guess it all depends," he said, "if those stories are true."

"What stories?" Alex asked right away. He was almost as young as Ty and was in his first year of scouting.

Eric turned away from the lake to face the boys. His mouth curved into a slow grin. "You mean nobody ever told you?" he asked.

"Stop fooling around, Eric," Mark snapped. "You're always trying to scare Ty. And this is a crummy time to make up a story."

"He's not making it up, Mark," Phil said in a low voice. "I heard Mr. Conklin and Mr. Anderson talking last night, too. They thought no one could overhear what they were saying. But Eric and I were hiding behind a tree."

"So what did they say?" Mark asked, sounding less confident.

"They said there was an old superstition about one of those islands," Eric said. "Something about a strange creature that lived on it."

"What kind of creature?" Ty asked, his eyes wide behind his thick glasses.

"They called it a shapeshifter," Phil answered.

"What's that mean?" Alex asked.

"Something like a werewolf, a creature that changes its shape from a human to a wolf," Eric said. "Mr. Anderson said there were old stories about a werewolf living on one of those islands."

Eric dropped his voice as the two scout leaders, Mr. Conklin and Mr. Anderson, came up to join the boys by the edge of the water.

"We're ready to push off, boys," Mr. Conklin said. "You have your packs ready?"

All six boys nodded.

"Any final questions before we get in the boat?" Mr. Anderson asked.

Alex raised his hand and started to say something. But Eric gave him such a mean look that he dropped his eyes and said, "Forget it."

"All right, then," Mr. Conklin said. "Let's run through the procedure one more time. We take you boys out onto the lake in the boats and then drop you off, one at a time, on the islands. You'll spend about thirteen hours alone out there, from 5:00 tonight 'til sunrise tomorrow morning. You have food, matches, and first aid supplies in your packs. You'll be using your sleeping bags without a tent tonight. Most important of all, each of you has two emergency flares. You can use them to signal us to come for you — but only in case of a serious emergency. Mr. Anderson and I will sleep in shifts tonight, so somebody will always be watching for the flares."

"And remember, Ty," Eric added when Mr. Conklin finished. "Being scared isn't an emergency."

The rest of the boys laughed nervously and started to pile their packs and sleeping bags into the two rowboats. Ty stared at Eric's back with hatred and checked a final time for the flares in his pack.

Mr. Anderson took out one of the boats with Phil, Mark, and Brad. Mr. Conklin rowed the other one with Eric, Alex, and Ty. The two boats skimmed through the water side by side halfway out to the islands. Then they parted, and the boys called out good-bye to each other.

Mr. Conklin rowed on toward the first island on the left side of the lake. It was a small, high island with a stand of fir trees in the middle. Ty looked at it and desperately hoped Mr. Conklin would tell him to get off there. But as the boat slid into the island's narrow beach, the leader ordered Alex to pick up his pack and go ashore. When the boat drew away again, Ty waved good-bye to Alex and caught the glimmer of fear in his eyes.

Mr. Conklin pulled the oars through the water toward the next island, which was larger and had more trees. But through the trees Ty could see a camping spot that looked out toward the base camp across the lake. It wasn't as safe-looking as Alex's island, but he wanted Mr. Conklin to give it to him.

"Okay, Ty, here's your island," Mr. Conklin said as the boat drew nearer.

Ty sighed with relief and reached for his pack. But Eric pushed his hand away.

"I want this island, Mr. Conklin," he said, glaring at Ty. "I have seniority in the troop. You owe it to me."

Mr. Conklin looked at Eric with irritation. "I think it's better if Ty stays here," he said. "I'm not sure he can handle the last island."

Eric grabbed his pack and sleeping bag and stood up in the boat.

"Too bad, Mr. Conklin," he said. "But I'm taking this island." Before the leader could stop him, Eric jumped into the shallow water and waded to shore. He ignored Mr. Conklin's shouts and ran up the hill to the open camping spot.

Ty felt a cold sweat break out over his body

as Mr. Conklin began to row the boat out toward the third island, which hulked like a dark creature in the lake.

"Sorry, Ty," Mr. Conklin said. "Eric shouldn't have taken that island. But there's nothing I can do about it now. I'm sure you'll be okay on the next one. Just use your flares if you need help."

Ty stared into the deep green water of the lake and thought how much he hated Eric. He wanted to ask Mr. Conklin to take him back to camp. But he knew the other scouts would call him a coward and never let him live it down.

The boat pulled closer and closer to the big island, where Ty had to spend the night. It was covered with thick trees and brush that made it impossible to see more than ten feet into the interior. Ty wondered if this was the island in the story. Maybe Eric knew that. Maybe that's why he jumped from the boat to make sure he didn't have to spend the night there.

"Mr. Conklin," Ty said, "is there something wrong with this place?" He stared straight into the leader's face. But Mr. Conklin wouldn't meet his eyes.

"Don't be ridiculous, Ty," he said. "It's just bigger than the rest. I didn't want you roaming around and getting lost on it, that's all. Find a camping place and stay there, okay? And make sure it's some place you can send flares from."

The boat slid onto the smooth rocks on the bottom of the shore around the island. Mr. Conklin reached out to give Ty a hand in getting out of the boat. Ty noticed that the leader's hand was cold and shaky, too.

"See you at 6:00 sharp, tomorrow morning," Mr. Conklin shouted as he pulled away in the boat. "And good luck."

Ty didn't move from the shore until the rowboat was just a tiny speck in the distance. Then he turned around and looked into the shadowy trees that crowded against each other on the island. He searched for a trail leading up from the beach into the trees, but thick bushes grew everywhere. Finally, he pushed through the undergrowth to a slight rise where the ground was clear except for long, matted grass.

Ty looked up and saw the gray fingers of twilight spreading across the sky. He knew he'd have to make camp soon. There was something about the clearing that he didn't like. It seemed unnatural in the middle of the thick trees, and there were animal bones strewn around in the long grass. But at least he could build a fire here. And the clearing was on the side of the island facing base camp. If he had to send flares off from here, at least the leaders could see them.

Ty went back into the shadowy woods to gather sticks and rocks for a fire. He had collected almost enough wood when he suddenly sensed that he wasn't alone. A chill ran down his spine like a warning signal. He picked up one final stick and ran back into the clearing.

As he pulled out pieces of the long grass to make a fire ring, Ty found more and more animal bones. He threw them aside in disgust and wondered if he should find a new campsite. But the sky had turned a deep midnight blue except where it was lit by the glow of the moon. Ty knew it was too late to go anywhere else. He'd have to make his fire and hope that it kept away whatever had eaten the flesh off those bones.

The leaping flames of the fire made Ty feel better. He pulled a sandwich from his pack and started to bite into it. But just then, a weird animal cry echoed through the trees. Ty dropped his food into the fire and jumped to his feet. The cry floated through the air again. It was the cry of an animal dying.

Fear rose up in Ty's stomach like a wave of nausea. He pulled his sleeping bag up closer to the fire. Once again, he checked his pack for the flares. Then he sat in the dark, listening and waiting.

The fire crackled as it devoured the dry sticks. Ty threw a few more on the flames and wished he had gathered a bigger supply. But now the woods were like a black wall around him. It was too late to go back for more sticks.

Ty felt his eyes growing heavy with sleep. But then he heard a sound in the trees behind him. It was the sound of footsteps dragging through the underbrush. The steps were heading toward the clearing and his fire.

With trembling hands, Ty reached into his backpack for the flares. Maybe they would scare away whatever was coming toward him. Maybe he could keep the thing far enough away until Mr. Conklin rowed across the lake to save him.

Ty was holding a match in one hand and a flare in the other when a figure stepped out of the woods into the light of his fire. At first, Ty gasped. Then he started to laugh with nervous relief.

Standing before him was another scout. Ty had never seen him before, but he was wearing a uniform just like the ones the older scouts in Ty's troop wore.

"I thought I was supposed to be alone on this island," the strange scout said, looking at Ty in surprise. "What are you doing here?"

Ty dropped the flare and stood up straight, trying to look confident. "Same thing you are,

I guess," he answered. "But you just about scared me to death."

"What did you think I was?" the older boy asked Ty, with a grin on his face.

"I . . . I don't know," Ty stammered.

"Well, I guess we'll have to share this campsite," he said, throwing his pack on the ground. "It's the only decent place to camp on the whole island. My name's Roger, by the way."

Ty smiled uneasily and introduced himself. "Have you ever done this before?" he asked Roger. "I mean, spent a night alone on an island."

"Lots of times," Roger said. "I guess you haven't."

"No, this is my first time," Ty admitted.

Roger grinned again and then crossed to the other side of the fire to unroll his sleeping bag. Ty watched as he opened his pack and pulled out a skinned rabbit.

"Where did you get that?" Ty asked, looking at the dead animal with disgust.

"I killed it," Roger said. "That's part of our special survival test. Don't you have to kill your own meat?"

"No," Ty said quietly. "I brought a sandwich, but I dropped it into the fire."

"It's a good thing I came along, then," Roger

said. "You might have starved to death 'til morning." He stuck a sharp stick through the rabbit's body. Then he held it over the fire to roast the meat. "You can have some of this."

Ty looked at the dead animal cooking over the flames and decided he'd rather go hungry. He hoped Roger wouldn't make a big deal out of him not eating it.

"Where are your scout leaders?" Roger asked, looking at Ty through the jumping flames.

"They're at base camp across the lake," Ty answered.

"So you're all alone here?" Roger asked.

"I was supposed to be," Ty said nervously. "Of course, you're here now."

Roger stared into the flames, turning the rabbit over on its other side. Ty watched his eyes glow in the reflected firelight.

"What's the matter? You look scared," Roger said, shifting his eyes to Ty. "What do you have to be scared about?"

"Nothing," Ty answered, his voice shaking. "I'm not scared."

Roger paused for a minute, and then he said in a lower voice, "I guess you haven't heard the story."

"What story are you talking about?" Ty asked nervously, moving closer to the fire.

"The story about this island," Roger said, turning around to look into the dark woods. "They say a shapeshifter lives here."

"That's just a scare story," Ty said. "I heard it from some guys in my troop." He was trying to seem calm, but the lump in his throat made his voice sound choked and frightened.

"Maybe you don't believe in shapeshifters," Roger said, cleaning off one of the bones and throwing it into the long grass.

"I don't know," Ty stammered.

"They could be real," Roger said. Then he looked at Ty and laughed.

Ty didn't laugh back. He was beginning to think he didn't like Roger.

"Have some meat," Roger said, tearing off a bloody leg from the rabbit and handing it to Ty.

Ty shrank away from it. His stomach was churning now, and the sight of the meat made him sick. "No, I'm not hungry," he said.

Roger chewed the meat off the bone and then threw it into the long grass. "But I'm still hungry," he said, staring at Ty. "Very hungry."

Ty felt fear creep through his body like a hot poison. Slowly, he reached back in the dark and tried to find the flares he'd dropped. But they were gone. Somehow, he'd lost them in the dark.

Roger finished the last bits of the rabbit. Then he got to his feet and gazed up at the full moon shining down on the campsite. A strange sound, like a growl, rose from deep in his throat. His face began to change shape and grow darker. Then, suddenly, Ty understood. He struggled to his feet, but it was too late.

Roger came at him from across the campsite. In the flickering firelight, Ty saw the hairy face and cruel eyes of the werewolf. He started to scream, but the werewolf kept coming, its sharp teeth bared and gleaming. Then Ty's screams suddenly stopped, and the island was still again in the middle of the deep, dark lake.

At sunrise the next morning, the scout leader searched and searched the island for Ty. But all he found was an empty campsite. And scattered in the long, matted grass he uncovered a set of human bones.